OUR GREATEST ENEMY

FIVE HORROR STORIES ON FATHERHOOD

JORDAN THIERY

To my father. I miss you, dad.

"My father used to play with my brother and me in the yard. Mother would come out and say, 'You're tearing up the grass.' 'We're not raising grass,' Dad would reply. 'We're raising boys.'"
–Harmon Killebrew

CONTENTS

OUR GREATEST ENEMY

BELT

10

"I cannot think of any need in children as strong as the need for a
father's protection." –Sigmund Freud

"Every father should remember one day his son will follow his
example, not his advice." –Charles Kettering

1

W illiam, at only twelve years old, felt perpetually stuck in an
in-between state, lost between the real and the imagined,
between living and simply surviving. He felt stuck between his father
and his mother, between happiness and boredom, between the past
and an unattainable future. He felt this strongly now, lost and unable
to traverse his memories, buckled in the passenger's seat of his father's
old, red pick-up truck.

Despite his confused state, he liked being in the truck. He liked
the truck for many reasons, but most of all because it was his father's
truck. It had a long bench seat, piled high with an assortment of

random things: pop bottles (some empty), candies (in this case a bag of licorice), sunflower seeds, piles of papers and receipts, and always his father's worn leather billfold. This wasn't everything, but it's what William keyed in on among the mess of other inessentials. Above his head, torn ceiling fabric dipped low and waved with the wind from his father's open window. William sometimes felt the urge to rip the fabric more, to see what was underneath, but held the temptation back. Tearing the fabric would make his father angry. His father drove the truck hard and didn't maintain it well, but neither did he encourage its decay. The truck's old frame shook violently on the gravel; despite years of neglect and rust, nuts and bolts held tight against the insistence of time. It wouldn't last forever, but it held up for now.

His father smoked a cigarette, the smoke forming a plume overhead, seasoning the aroma of the interior. The trapped air inside the cab always held a mixture of fresh burning tobacco smoke and the stale burn that clung to the upholstery. The smell was not only the smell of the truck, but had become distinctly his father's smell. It made William feel content and relaxed. He knew the smoke was poison, because his father told him it was, but that didn't matter. It was his father's smell. He watched as his father pinched the filter of the cigarette, removed it from his lips, and flicked the finished butt out the window. Some of the ashes were caught by the wind, orange embers scattering back into the cab. His father's gaze remained settled out the front of the truck and the blackness ahead of them.

William loved his father, his gray hair and deeply tanned skin, his bright blue eyes contrasted with dry, red lines and a yellowness he didn't understand. His father's neck and cheeks were covered with a scruffy morning shadow, a stubble that always tickled his cheeks when his father picked him up. He was a brute, a real man, a beacon of strength and willpower. William felt ashamed in his father's presence, as if he wasn't worthy of having him as his father. William was small. William was weak. William wasn't good at much of anything. He wanted to be just like his father, wanted his father to be proud of him, but felt the goal unobtainable, forever out of reach.

Then he thought about his mother, his kind and patient mother, who wasn't in the truck with them. Her absence wasn't exactly uncommon (these late night drives were only meant for him and his father), but he couldn't remember where his mother was. He couldn't remember where he'd last seen her. This was the part that was weird, the aspect of the drive that bothered him.

"Dad, where is mom?" He asked.

"She was a bitch, William. Just us right now. Leave it at that," his father said.

The response confused William and he wanted to ask more. His parents were clearly fighting again (a fight was always the catalyst for a late night drive), and his father would eventually vent and complain about things, would get angry, yell, and then they'd go home. Yet the gaps in his memory continued to nag at him, to alarm him. He had a disjointed memory of being carried out of the house by his father, but nothing about his mother. How long ago had they left the house exactly?

He was tired, he decided, which was why his memory was hazy. He let it go. For now, at least. His father would tell him more when he was ready. Or William would figure it out on his own, which was something he had to do sometimes. He picked up on more than his parents gave him credit for; they'd talk about things in code while he was in his room, but William always knew exactly what they were talking about.

From the middle of the bench seat, William picked up the bag of licorice. The bag was unopened. His mouth watered as he thought about the red sticks, already tasting the cherry flavor, the oddly satisfying rubber texture. He wanted to eat a piece but wasn't sure about being the one to open the bag. Not until his father opened the bag, at least. Sometimes his father was weird about things like that, as if opening something that wasn't his was a sign of disrespect. He looked up at his father, who was still focused on driving. Would he notice if William tore that bag open slowly? William was tempted, but ultimately decided it wasn't worth the risk. He set the unopened bag back down.

William knew his father cared about him. At least, he was pretty sure he did. His father had high expectations was all and that's why he could be mean and rough sometimes. It was a tough love. He knew that's what it was because little things would give it away, like his father's insistence that he never smoke cigarettes. They were bad for him his father would explain, poisonous and addicting. His father was open, reflective, and insistent that William never "pick up the habit." In William's mind, if his father didn't care, he wouldn't care what William did to his body. Even with this warning from his father, William would secretly enjoy the smell whenever he could. He'd breathe in the burning aroma with delight, the initial lighting of a new cigarette always being the best. It stung his nose a bit breathing it in, but after that passed, it felt so, so good. It was the smell of his father, after all.

William looked out his window. It was dark outside with nothing to look at but the blur of trees beyond the ditch. In the silence, his mind eventually wandered back home to his mother and the gaps in his memory. Why couldn't he remember anything? The thought was annoyingly insistent. The night seemed to have no beginning; being in the truck felt as if it were the beginning of time, as if it had always been that way, as if he'd been born in the very seat he sat in. He pushed himself to think, as hard as he could, and a series of distinct moments came to him, of being rushed out of the house, the slapping of the screen door, the truck engine turning over in the quiet night. But these were snapshots without collective meaning. The temptation to ask his father questions festered like itchy hands, as if he'd played with the exposed wall insulation at home.

"Dad," William said cautiously, "I would like to know what's going on. At least something. Can you tell me anything?"

"William, not right now. Just wait. Sit quietly and wait. I need to think."

And that was that. William retreated again. He was fearful that something bad had happened, and was struggling to keep himself under control. He could barely hear his thoughts over the beating of his heart, a deep echo that reverberated outward from his chest, quicker, quicker, faster, faster. He felt like an animal sensing certain doom, head poked above the tall grass, contemplating escape. But he couldn't run. He was trapped in the moving truck, trapped in between states as he always was.

He reminded himself of what his mother would say whenever he was worked up. "Just breathe," she'd say, "Deeply. Then breathe again. Take deep breaths until your heart slows down." As he remembered her words, he listened to them, taking a deep breath. Then he took another. Then another. They were deep breaths that filled the entirety of his lungs. Eventually he did feel better, could at least think somewhat straight.

He looked up at his father and noticed something new in his eyes. His father usually bore the distant look of someone without care for anything in the world, or fury whenever he was mad. At that moment, however, the look was different.

Was it the look of hurt?

Regret?

Sadness?

Maybe it was a mix of all those things at once. There was a wetness on the edges of his father's eyes, as if he were on the verge of tears. But they couldn't be tears. He'd never seen his father cry. When his father was upset, the only emotion William ever saw was anger, vengeful rage and raw power. Were they watering from the burning smoke of the cigarette? It had to be that.

Everything was okay, he decided. Soon, his father would begin talking about how selfish his mother was, about how she didn't care about anyone but herself. Eventually his mother would call and ask where they were, that it was getting late, that William had school in the morning, and they'd go home.

School.

Did he have school tomorrow? What day was it, exactly? When had he last been to school? And why was everything so goddamn *fuzzy*? He looked around the truck for his father's cell phone to check the date and time, maybe see if his mother had called. He was careful not to move anything, didn't want his father asking what he was doing. He glanced through the cluttered mess but couldn't find the phone. His father usually set it on the bench seat next to his wallet, but it wasn't there. His chest thumped harder, and with each thump words circled in his mind:

Where is my mother? What is going on?

Where is my mother? What is going on?

Where is my mother and *what is going on!?*

In response, his mother's voice in his mind: Stop. Deep breath. Relax. Deep breath. Think. Deep breath. So he listened to her again, and it began to work. He put his hand on his chest and could feel the pounding inside slow down, weaken. *Alright*, he said to himself. *Back to routine. There's nothing new here, nothing weird. Just another late night drive calming dad down.* He looked down at his feet, hanging above the trash-filled floor of the passenger seat. He saw his feet for the first time that night. They were streaked with what was probably mud (he couldn't really tell in the dark, but what else could it be?) and he didn't have shoes on. Surely they didn't rush out of the house so fast that they didn't grab shoes. He saw the rest of his body, saw that he was in his pajamas, as if he'd been pulled from his bed. They must have left the house in a hurry.

Feeling overwhelmed, he laid his head against the cool window, covered his head with his arms, and sought peace through sleep and darkness.

2

The rushing wind beat against the side of the vehicle and woke William. He rubbed the coolness from the side of his face touching the glass. He sluggishly watched the blurring lines of trees that whipped by from his window as he awoke. He couldn't see any individual trees as the rows blended together. Each row was broken by a brief period of blackness, where the gravel roads cut through them before the next row of trees began. He knew that beyond the trees were fields for farming, even if he couldn't see them in the night. He remembered those rows of trees bordering farmer's fields being called windbreaks, or sometimes shelterbelts. His grandfather had explained their purpose to him at one point in time, trees planted after the "dust bowl" to prevent dust storms from happening again. William didn't really understand what the "dust bowl" was, only that it was a bad thing from before he was born, but the purpose of the trees protecting the farmer's fields was clear.

He imagined the rows of trees in his mind on a sunny day, the branches rustling, trunks waving back and forth as brutal Midwestern winds battered them. The winds would blow hard against one side of the trees, and they would stand in unison, bending in one direction but hindering the power behind those great winds. The wood would creak, some branches would snap and fall, but the farmland soil on the other side, seeds planted and awaiting germination, would remain undisturbed. Some trees would crack and fall, many would die, but seeds would fall and new trees would grow in their place. Then, as winds shifted, as winds always do, the trees would bend the other way and protect the plot of land on the other side.

The shelterbelts, now generations old, continued to prevent the fields and the farmers from destruction, even if that history of their purpose was long forgotten.

His grandfather would talk about his fear of history being forgotten by the younger farmers coming in. The shelterbelts weren't immortal, he'd say, didn't always self-sustain. They had to be cared for, cleaned up, new trees grown in the gaps where new seeds hadn't taken root. Some farmers had begun tearing the trees down row by row, eager to take advantage of the soil underneath and the profit it would translate into. He could sense, he'd tell William, that winds were beginning to grow stronger over the years, even if he couldn't prove it. What would happen when all the shelterbelts were cut down? Would that "dust bowl" come again? Would they be equipped to recover?

William missed his grandfather. It had been lonely since he'd passed, and his parents fought more because of it. He had been small in stature but big in heart, stepping in when the fighting was especially bad, as if he'd been doing it since both William's parents were young adults. His grandfather would often nurture his mother, tell her to calm down, tell her to speak her mind in kinder ways, ways that wouldn't rip and tear at his father's pride. Then he'd speak to his father about respecting women, would help ease some of the pressure from his shoulders, would tell him that it's okay to show weakness sometimes and that he didn't always need to be right. Everyone needed something, and his grandfather knew exactly the thing for each person. He was an expert at calming tumultuous storms.

But now he was gone, half a year under the ground. There was a vacancy. Grain by grain, undisturbed soil was being lifted, the air becoming harder to see through, with only William to stand in between.

William put his hand against the frigid glass of the window. It wasn't winter yet, but late fall, that short window of time where it almost hurt to be outside, but not enough yet for bulky clothing. There was no snow on the ground to play in, only the awfully bitter wind. He removed his hand and tried to turn around to look out the back window, but his seat belt held him in place. He unbuckled. From out back he saw town as nothing but a scattering of dots far off on the horizon, lights etching across the sky. A plume of dust obscured most of the road, and he wondered when they'd last been on pavement. He could only remember gravel. To leave town, they would have taken the interstate for some time, but he couldn't remember that far back. He must have been asleep.

A rock hit the window at his side, making a sharp *tink* and startling him. He turned to face the front again.

"Buckle up, William. I don't want you to get hurt," his father said.

William clicked his seat belt back on.

Fog was forming ahead of them. He found it creepy to look at, especially driving through it. Fog made William feel as if he were perpetually stuck in place, as if everything around him was stuck in limbo.

"Dad, the fog is so weird," he said, attempting to break the silence because he was tired of the quiet, of nothing happening.

"Mhm," was all his father said.

His father picked up the bag of seeds from the middle of the seat, poured a handful into one hand, resting his arm on the steering wheel to continue guiding the vehicle. He popped the seeds into his mouth and set the bag back down, making sure not to spill.

William tried to think of something else to talk about. "I think I'd like to take my bike out tomorrow. After school, maybe," is what he decided on.

"Probably not, William."

"Why not? Maybe we can go buy roller blades, dad. I've wanted to try rollerblading for a long time now." William paused, allowing his father time to respond. When he didn't, William continued, "I think I'd really like that. I'd like to do that with you, dad."

His father smiled and nodded. "Of course, bud."

William's head was pulsing. He wanted his dad to talk, to complain about something, anything to end the never-ending silence of the endless drive. "Will mom meet us where we're going?" He asked, hoping to force the issue.

"No," his father said, and then said nothing more.

William stared at his father, waiting for more. Seconds passed and it became clear no response was coming. "Why not?" William asked, sensing irritation in his own voice. *Be careful*, a voice inside his mind said, a part of him that didn't want his father to direct the anger at him. Anger at his mother was fine, normal, but not anger at him.

"The bitch is gone, William. Fuck her. Fuck. Her. Enough talking. Be quiet."

Okay, William thought, but didn't say, his voice caught by his father's harshness.

Had his parents finally gotten divorced? William often wondered when this would happen. Because of all the fighting, he counted on it happening some day, had an internal bet that it would be once he was done with school. But he wasn't done with school yet, and things were happening too fast. If they had divorced it seemed too sudden. Wouldn't there be more to it? He didn't know what the process involved, but it didn't seem like something his parents could decide and do while William was asleep. Wouldn't he have said goodbye to his mother? Wouldn't there be some sort of agreement for when he'd see her again?

He stopped his thoughts from continuing down a bad path and took a deep breath. He didn't want his parents to be divorced. He saw them happy, too. Talking, smiling, laughing. His mother looking up at his father with a beam of affection that made William envious for a partner of his own someday. The fighting couldn't overshadow that. They always got over it. They would continue to get over it until they were both old and too tired to fight anymore.

Looking out his side window again, abandoning the mission with his father, William watched as they passed a cross section. The gravel road was lit up briefly by the headlights as they passed, another side road leading nowhere.

3

The night was getting darker, the fog thicker and heavier. The fog seemed to be growing thick enough that the trees and ditches at the sides of the road were being consumed into nothingness. Soon they wouldn't be able to see the road in front of them at all, he figured. William's father had turned on the brights, which hadn't helped much, and may have made things worse. No other vehicle had passed them yet, which given the late hour of the night made sense. It was only the never ending gravel road ahead of them, his father never stopping or turning, simply maintaining the same speed endlessly forward.

"Dad, we've been driving all night," William said.

"Just wait." his father said.

William felt pain in his neck, probably from sitting in the same position for so long. He shifted into a new position. His father took up a bottle of pop lying beside the bag of seeds and opened it. The fizz sharply hissed out of the opening. He took a deep drink of the bottle then finished it by flashing his teeth and shaking his head. Why he did that, William had no idea. His father was an odd man sometimes, but he loved him so much.

"You know, William," his father unexpectedly said.

William perked up, excited for something. Anything to pass the endless, uncertain silence.

"Women are always hell. You know that, right?"

"Yes, I know, dad," William said. He was ready to be his father's confidant, his best friend. It was the role he was meant to play.

"Do you think it's fair, the way she treated me?" He asked.

William considered his words, methodically removing some and adding others in his mind before he spoke. If this conversation made it back to his mother, he'd have to be able to spin it as neutral, but he still needed his father to know at that moment that William was on his side.

"I don't know what happened tonight, dad, but yes, sometimes we can all be a little mean to each other."

"Sometimes I feel like I have weak skin, that I should have been able to man up and take it. But I was just so tired of it, all the little daggers. She just doesn't stop."

"I know, dad."

"I mean, if she cared about me, would she be so cruel?"

William could think of no response, so he stayed quiet, hopeful that his father would simply continue on his own. His father did.

"You know, before your mom and I met, when I was still dating other people, sometimes I was mean to people. Here's the thing about that. Do you know what that meant, when I was mean to those girls?" His father asked, looking at William.

William shook his head.

"It meant I didn't really like them. It meant I felt like I could say and do whatever I wanted, and they wouldn't go anywhere, because I had them under my thumb. I was mean to them because I could be mean. I remember that and I wonder, is that what your mom thinks of me? An inconsequential toy?"

William thought maybe his father was being a little dramatic, but he also understood it. His mother could be harsh, and sometimes seemed to relish the opportunity for a fight. However, at the same time, William thought about all the times his father called his mother a "useless bitch", and thought that maybe it was all a bit more complicated, a little too complicated for him to fully understand. There were layers that lead to the cruelty.

His father sighed deeply. "I've been sitting here thinking about if I made the right choice. If I should have stayed. In the end, I don't think it would have mattered."

"Dad, you're just mad right now. We'll go home when everything calms down," William said, because that's how it always was.

His father ignored his answer. William was only a sounding board, after all. His father didn't need his help making decisions and he accepted that. He just wanted to go home, and the faster his father got this out of his system, the faster they'd turn around.

"I just don't understand why," his father said.

"I don't know dad. I don't think mom means it. I think she's just tired and wants to fight."

"So that makes it okay?"

William tensed. He'd gotten sloppy, had said the wrong thing. His words had made it sound like he was on his mother's side. "Well, no, I just..."

"She needs a goddamn therapist," his father interrupted.

William thought they both did, but couldn't say that. He didn't know what to say. "Maybe we should go home and talk to her about it," he said, hopeful.

His father looked at him and his expression changed, as if he realized or remembered something, because his eyes went wide and his lips parted slightly. William thought he looked scared. The look unsettled William because it didn't fit his father's face. His father wasn't scared of anything. William felt a sudden urge to open the truck door and escape. He wanted to hide in the trees, sheltered from the wind, imagining his grandfather's embrace. Tears were forming in the corners of his own eyes as he started to feel helpless and trapped. He looked away from his father and back out the front window, trying to lose himself in the image of the rolling fog.

4

A long time seemed to pass in silence before his father spoke again.

"Have I ever told you how your mother and I met?" his father asked.

William thought this was an odd thing to talk about, but it was better than their last conversation. He *had* been curious about it, but had never asked. To him, his parents were like the beginning of the universe: Life began with their relationship already intact, and anything before that moment was untraceable. William had a hard time imagining his mother and father being young, of them being raised by their own parents. Like a bomb in his mind, William wondered if his father had these same conversations with his father. The thought lingered for a bit before he shook it from his mind with a shudder. He couldn't handle that. It was all too cyclical.

His father was smiling. "I was a Senior in high school and she was a Junior," he said, "We grew up somewhere a long way from here. Both of us were from small towns, not like where we live now. Where we lived, these small towns had a few thousand people each and were fairly close to each other. Maybe a fifteen to twenty minute drive from town to town. I'm jumping ahead a bit, but mom and I moved when you were very little to be where we live now, where we could both make more money. I'm not sure now if that was the best idea, but it was better for you to be in a bigger school. You've always been so smart. It was important to us to provide something better for you in that way." His father paused, mulling something over. "But I think it might have cost us something, too. I'm not sure how to explain it. It's harder here. Stressful. Faster. Chaotic. Maybe the city got the best of us. Maybe we weren't bred for it.

"Anyway. When we were in high school, in those smaller towns, we'd often get together with nearby towns to party or socialize. Just to see different people. My graduating class only had twenty people in it, you see, so we kind of get tired of seeing the same people. And it got a little weird after break ups and the number of new people available to sleep with started to slim down. Well, I had gone to this party outside the town where your mom grew up. We were both at this party with friends, drinking around a campfire in the country. We had our cars, cars were a big deal for us back then, and they'd all be parked in a line. Some people would be hanging out by the fire, some would be checking out cars or leaning against them. We'd be there until two or three in the morning before we all staggered out of there and went home again. I miss that, William, that simpler time."

His father stopped to take a shaky breath before continuing.

"So anyway, I've got a crowd of people around me and my car, see I had a firebird that I had to sell when you were born. A really beautiful car. But I see your mom by the bonfire. Your mother is beautiful, just this gem of a person, and I'm mystified by her. She has these long brown curls and this beautiful smile. She's got a few friends around her, but she's glowing, right. I can't see anyone but her. I walked away from my group, went up to her and said 'hey,' and she just says 'hey' and turns back to her friends kind of giggling, all shy. I ask her to go on a walk with me, and she says sure, and we just started walking down the road. We talked all night. I'd never been so content with just talking to someone as I had been that night with your mom. It felt meant to be. We started to date. She didn't have a car so I'd always pick her up and take her places to talk and hang out. What we had was so beautiful back then, while we dated."

William watched as a couple tears dripped from the corners of his father's eyes. His father's lips curled up into a hint of a smile and he sat like that was for a short time before his face grew stern and the smile disappeared.

"But it doesn't last, bud. Something happened to us. Maybe it was because we stopped spending time on ourselves, started spending too much time at work. Maybe we never learned how to really talk to each other when stress started building. Maybe things boiled over when your grandpa died. I don't know, I really don't. If I did, I think I could have fixed it. I wish I could take it all back. I'd tell her, 'Let's stay here. We don't need to move.' But I don't think it would have mattered. Your mom was insistent. It probably isn't that simple, either. Maybe we were destined to fight wherever we ended up. Maybe the move didn't have anything to do with it all. Maybe I'm using it as an excuse, and things always become corrupt, because that's what we all eventually become, but, God! To go back in time and try something else. Anything. I wish your mom's smile would light my world on fire again, that I could go back and find out what broke us."

His father stopped and looked in the rear view mirror. He cleared his throat, wiped his eyes, and gathered himself.

"The thing is, I don't want this to happen to you. I know you saw how much we fought, and I don't want that for you. Marriage... It always goes to hell at some point. It's unavoidable. It happened to my parents. I still remember dad locking mom out of the house, telling her to go fuck herself, to go spend the night with one of her boyfriends. That image is burned in my memory. I didn't want that for you. But now it doesn't matter. It doesn't matter because we've already burned those images in your mind, and there's no erasing them. I'm so sorry, William."

"It's okay, dad," William said, not knowing what he was supposed to say.

There were more tears on his father's face, filling the wrinkles around his eyes and shining against the neon dashboard of the truck.

"I messed up, William," his father said, "I messed up so bad." His father's knuckles were white from gripping the steering wheel.

Without warning, the silence of the truck was shattered by his father's scream. It was a scream that made William's own throat hurt by the rawness of it, knowing how it must have torn at his father's vocal cords. It was a scream William felt in his bones. William was staring at his father wide-eyed, unsure of what to do, was shrinking into himself, cowering, hiding. His father didn't stop after that first scream, only took in more air to follow it with a second scream, this one lasting until his voice sounded scratchy and hoarse. William didn't want to exist in the moment anymore, wanted to disappear forever. His father's hands were shaking on the steering wheel, the truck was moving faster now, everything outside whipping by at blinding speeds.

William buried his face into his knees and closed his eyes, wishing it all away.

"Dad, please take me home," William begged, "I want to see mom."

His father's screaming became a whimper, and William could feel the truck slowing down. William didn't leave the cocoon of his lap. This was all his fault.

5

William wasn't sure if he was dreaming, but it felt like he was dreaming. In the darkness of his solitude, head in his lap, he played Jenga with his mother and father. They took turns removing the blocks slowly. His father was methodical. He took one of his big paws, curled into a fist, pinky extended. He found a middle block near the bottom of the tower, and poked it gently with his extended pinky. Poke, poke, poke, until half of the block emerged from the other side. He smiled at William, who looked up at his impressive father with a smile and watched as he pulled the block out with ease. His father set the block on the top of the pile and looked at his mother. It was her turn.

His mother, never one to take her time, quickly grabbed the side of a block halfway up the tower and pulled it free. The tower wobbled back and forth, back and forth, then settled back into place. His father looked at her with shock and wide eyes before letting out a sigh of relief. William laughed. His mother smiled, happy with the reaction she'd achieved. She set her block down on the top of the pile.

It was William's turn. He was nervous. There were so many blocks. He touched a few of them, unsure of which decision to make, as each block felt too sturdy to pull. Finally he decided. He tried to be still like his father, but he couldn't help but shake. It frustrated him, the way his hands shook. He pushed the chosen block through, then gripped it from the other side as it was exposed. He pulled. The tower leaned. His father gently held the side of the tower, preventing it from toppling. He looked at William and nodded his head, a nod that said *hurry* and William did. The block came free. The tower stood still as his father removed his hands from the side of the tower. William grinned up at his father, who was surely so, so proud of him now.

His mother, always one eager for action, pushed the tower over quickly. Blocks scattered everywhere with a crash. Both William and his father leapt back in shock. His father looked at his mother with narrowed eyes, but she was smiling. She was only playing, William knew, in her own way. William looked at the pile of broken tower pieces for a moment before starting to giggle. As he laughed, his mother and father smiled, and they built the tower back up for another game.

6

"I hit her, William." His father said, breaking the silence of the truck.

William lifted his head and opened his eyes. The neon glow of the dashboard blurred like millions of stars as his eyes adjusted to the light. His father was tapping the steering wheel softly with his palm as he spoke.

"I got too mad, I got too into it, and I hit her. Do you understand, William? There's no going back from that. That's the end of the road. For me, for us. I can't fix that."

The word *hit* seemed to unlock a door in William's mind, and chunks of memory slowly returned. He remembered his parents yelling in the kitchen while he sat on the stairs around the corner, waiting for things to calm down. He'd left his bed when he'd heard their voices and came down the stairs to investigate. William didn't know what the fight was about, but he never really knew. In his mind every fight seemed like the same one rehashed from last time, with the words in a different order. As he peeked around the corner he saw his mother pointing a finger at his father, then jabbing it into his chest. He remembered his father use the word that always made him cringe: *bitch*.

No dad, he'd thought. Never that word. Never call anyone that word. That's the worst, most vile word.

His mother slapped his father. Time seemed to stand still as the two of them stared at each other, his mother's eyes burning fury, his father's full of shock. Then his father changed. Quickly he transitioned from surprise, to confusion, then hurt, then anger. He hit back but harder and with a closed fist. He remembered his mother's head rock with the impact, bending too far to one side, far enough to not be natural. Time stood still again as she fell. He remembered the vibrations in the floor as her body collapsed with several dull thuds. He remembered blood.

He shook away the memory. *No, that's not real,* he told himself. *She's okay. She's fine. It was a hit, but she's only a little hurt. She'll be fine. Everything will be fine.*

"You only did it once, Dad," he told his father.

"It doesn't matter, William. It only takes once. It only ever takes once when it's something like that."

His father was looking at him, frantic chaos in his eyes, wet and red with agitation and terror. The truck was swerving on the gravel, and he noticed that his father was less in control, the wheel sliding carelessly through his fingers.

"Someday, William, you'll know what I mean. There are moments in your life where everything changes. Sometimes it's for the better, like when you were born. My life changed, and I gained something more important than I ever could have imagined. But there are also bad moments, too. Moments where you make a mistake, a mistake that you can't return from. Some mistakes aren't two way doors, William, doors you can apologize for crossing and step back through. Sometimes you step through the doorway and you don't like where you wandered, but it doesn't matter. Once you cross the threshold, you have to accept it. And I... I can't accept what I've done.

"When I was little, I watched my dad beat my mom. He'd scream at her with a blood red face, blame her for things that weren't her fault, and I always thought: Not me. Never me. I'll be better... Fuck!" His father hit the steering wheel with a closed fist. He hit it again and again in rapid succession. William wondered if the steering wheel could snap off. His father was so strong.

There was a brief pause, an ominous silence, and William didn't know what to do. His father grabbed the half-empty pop bottle he'd drunk earlier, the unfortunate thing closest to him, and threw it at the windshield. The plastic cap broke as it connected with the glass and the liquid escaped, spraying William's face and eyes and caking the front seat. William wiped it from the corners of his eyes as it stung.

"William... William I'm so sorry," his father said, reaching out to him to help wipe it off.

William only stared at his clothes. His shirt and pants were soaked. He'd be sticky after it dried. He hated being sticky. He hated being unclean.

"You'll dry off. I'll turn on the air."

"Can we just stop somewhere so I can change," William asked.

"It doesn't work like that. You'll be okay. I'm sorry."

William went back to wiping himself off the best he could. He wanted new clothes. "Dad, where are we?" he asked.

"William, I don't know. Please stop asking because I don't know."

He looked up at his father. "What do you mean?" He asked.

"I mean I don't know where we are or where we're going."

"Dad, I'm done," William said, "I want to go home."

"William, when you came down stairs, did you see your mom?" His father asked, changing the subject.

William thought about pushing back, about not letting his father get away from his question, but decided he didn't care enough to fight it. "I saw, but I don't remember much," he said. It was a lie. He remembered seeing his mother's body on the floor, but he didn't want to remember it. The pain in William's neck was getting worse, more intense. It throbbed now, demanding attention. Why did it hurt so bad? He put his hand up to feel it. When he took the hand away to look, it came back full of blood. He wiped the blood on his pajama pants.

"I grabbed you as you ran at her," his father said, "I'm not sure I knew what I was doing."

William remembered being on the stairs, looking around the corner into the kitchen to see his father with his fist still in the air, his mother on the ground. He remembered the low guttural moan escaping from his father. His father's hand was no longer a fist, instead reaching out to his mother on the floor. William hadn't been sure if he should comfort his father or his mother at that moment. He was never really sure. His legs guided him from the stairs into the kitchen.

The driver's side window cracked under his father's fist and William jumped in his seat at the sound of it. "Why would I do that, William? Why did I hurt her? Why couldn't I stop myself?" His father hit the window a few more times, then placed his hand back on the wheel. His knuckles were shining with his own blood.

"I don't know, dad."

Things had followed a normal pattern up to this point. His parents would fight, they would vent, and they would move on. Why were things escalating now? Maybe that was how these things always progressed. Maybe these things were destined for continual escalation, like a drug.

"Dad?" William had asked when he rounded the corner and into the kitchen. He'd seen his father, lying there on his mother's body, crying. His mother's eyes closed, her body unmoving. William knelt down beside them both, touched his mother's cheek. It was warm. "Mom? Mom, please wake up."

"William, close your eyes," his father had said. William didn't want to, but he did as he was told. Now blind, he felt himself swept up and rushed through the house, heard the smack of the screen door as it shut behind them, felt the cold air against his calves because his pants had scrunched up when his father picked him up, heard the rusty truck door creaking open as he was dropped onto the bench seat.

"Buckle up, bud," his father had said as he shut the door.

He'd buckled. His father had gotten in next and slammed his door. His father had started the truck, had looked back at the screen door as lights filtered out from inside the house. He'd seemed to pause there for a moment, looking at the light from the door, everything around them too quiet. Then his father had taken out his cell-phone, dialed a number, and put the phone to his ear. William had heard a muffled voice answer on the other end, to which his father had said, "Please send help. My wife is hurt, she hit her head." He'd given the address and hung up.

They'd sat in the truck for a while, his father sitting, thinking, and William unsure of what was happening.

Eventually his father had backed out of the driveway.

7

His father slowed the truck and parked. Surprisingly, they'd reached a dead end. They could only go left or right now. The left turn was still covered in the dense, dark fog. It seemed to roll angrily, as if it were a living wall of blackness. On the right, however, the fog cleared, and William could see as far as the truck lights reached through the darkness beyond that path.

"Get out of the truck, William," his father said.

William, sensing what his father was doing, refused. "I want to go with you, dad," he said.

William's gaze was still fixated on the fog to the left, so perfectly ugly. He was okay with that fog. He was okay with being lost in it, as long as he was with his father.

"Bud, you mean so much to me, and I want you to know that."

"Dad–" William started to say, but couldn't finish.

He was being squeezed. His father had reached across the bench seat, which he could do because he wasn't buckled, and he was hugging him deeply, making it somewhat hard to breathe. It was always awkward hugging his father, like there was some unspoken rule that men shouldn't show affection. Yet his father, the creator of that unspoken rule, had his arms wrapped tightly around him, squeezing harder than he'd ever done before. William raised his free arm around his father and hugged back. From behind him, William heard the door lever being pulled. The door creaked open and he was pushed out.

He hit the ground hard and felt needles up his back as the gravel dug into his skin.

"I love you, William," his father said before slamming the passenger door shut. William tried to jump up, but the pain in his neck stopped him, and he reached back and held it. The tires spun dirt and gravel up into William's face as his father drove off into the dark fog. He watched the vehicle speed away, a plume growing behind it.

I love you, William. The words repeated in his head over and over. He desperately wanted to say them back, but now he couldn't. His father was gone, had taken away the opportunity from him. His father was his everything, his world view. Without his father he had nothing and no direction, would spend the rest of his life wandering aimlessly for approval that no one could give. He felt more lost than he'd ever felt before.

He stood and screamed at the truck for as long as he could, long after he couldn't see it anymore, calling for him to come back to him, to help him, that he could do better, that he could be like grandpa if he gave him the chance. But it was no use. His father wasn't returning. The truck had long since disappeared into the fog. William collapsed back onto the gravel. For the first time in his life, he didn't only feel alone, he was truly alone. He didn't want to be alone. He didn't know what he wanted.

When he felt some strength return, he stood, and began walking down the path on the right.

8

He remembered waking up in the ditch beside the highway, the blur of flashing red and blue lights, people running and yelling. He'd felt cold, deeply cold, into his bones, as if he'd spent the last few hours under-dressed in the freezing night. He was lifted out of the ditch and placed on a stretcher. His neck, head, and body were secured onto the mobile bed by a paramedic, as others rolled him away from the ditch. He'd learn later that they'd feared his neck was broken, feared that he was paralyzed, but the injury was minor and quick to heal. After a two-week hospital stay, he'd leave the hospital just fine. Physically at least.

While he hadn't been able to move his head on the stretcher, he'd at least been able to look out across the ditch. At first he couldn't quite make out what it was in the dark, but as his eyes adjusted, and as the lights flashed against the object, he saw what was left of his father's truck. A twisted heap of scrap, nothing more than a crumpled ball of metal. He hadn't seen it clearly back then, but he would later see the images online, and they'd haunt him. He would stare at those images for years as he became a teenager, then eventually a young adult. He'd search for answers in the images, answers to where his father had gone.

Buckle up, William. I don't want you to get hurt, his father had said earlier that night, and how prophetic those words had been. His father's busted and broken body would be found far beyond the vehicle. There were no images of the body, but the coroner had left detailed notes. At the time, just a child lying on a stretcher, he hadn't yet known where his father had gone. He desperately searched for him in the darkness beyond the wreckage.

As he searched, he listened to his mother's squealing words beside him.

"William," she'd said, "Oh baby, you're awake, oh thank God."

Thank God, he'd thought to himself. *There is no God. Not there. Not here.*

She'd placed her free hand on the side of his head and kissed his forehead. The affection hurt, and the paramedics asked her to be careful.

William, still looking out into the night, had asked, "Mom, where's dad?" He searched, and he asked, and he searched, and he asked. Over and over that night, and for years after. But all he saw out there beyond the wreckage was the row of trees along the highway, the shelterbelt. Each branch of every tree in that belt had been still and unmoving, everything calm. Useless.

9

As he'd grown, people would tell William that the drive had been nothing more than the dream of an unconscious child, lying hurt and cold in the ditch following the accident, waiting for help to arrive. But that wasn't true at all. William knew it had been real, that he'd spent a brief moment of time with his father's soul. His father had tried to save him from death, had pushed him out of the truck and back onto the path of the living.

Instead, he'd sent William's cold and lifeless body stumbling home, his soul forever stuck, wandering that gravel road, searching, and asking, and searching, and asking.

William stared down at the woman below him, the *bitch*, her head looking like a burst watermelon. His fists were covered in her blood. She would likely die, but there was still a chance. Her chest rose and fell with slow breathing, a soft wind escaping through her nose.

He couldn't allow her to live. He stood and removed the belt from his pants. He felt the leather, smooth and taut. The belt was strong.

He wrapped the belt around the woman's neck and pulled. He pulled hard. It took some time, but eventually she did wake, looking up at him in wide-eyed horror. Still he pulled, as her body wriggled underneath the belt. The belt did not break. It bent and swayed with her movements, but the belt did not break.

Eventually her movements ceased. He held the belt for a few minutes longer, her body still, her dead eyes still staring into his. He held the belt tight until he was certain there was no more wind inside her lungs.

He stared at her for a while, seeing a woman he may have cared about at one time. The woman's belly squirmed. William watched as it moved, knowing it would soon stop. There was still death ahead of them, a second life to eliminate to fully terminate the cycle.

"I did it, dad," he whispered into the quiet room with pride. "It's over."

He closed his eyes and breathed in deeply. Then he placed his hand on the woman's belly, still waiting for the movement beneath to end. He began to cry once the quakes of life did cease, as he stared into the blackness behind his eyelids.

"Are you proud of me?" He asked the silence.

He expected no answer. Not yet at least. He awaited his judgment, waited to join his father in that place beyond the endless purgatory of the living.

WRAPPED IN SILK

20

"The nature of impending fatherhood is that you are doing something that you're unqualified to do, and then you become qualified while doing it." –John Green

"It is easier to build strong children than to repair broken men." –Frederick Douglass

1

The pattering of warm water echoed against the walls of the tight shower as Erik stared up at a black spider above the shower head, resting in the corner of the ceiling where the walls met. It had made a thick web that spanned across the corner and sat in front of a hole in the web that disappeared into the ceiling tile. Its eight arching legs were unsettlingly long, and Erik could see sharp, black bristles along each of those thin legs, could see the water reflecting back at him off of the spider's many eyes. The eyes of the spider stared down at him as he stared up at it. The spider's appearance in such a vulnerable place, so close to his face, body completely nude, made Erik's skin tickle. He shivered with unease despite the warmth of the hot shower water.

Up until he'd seen the spider, he'd been enjoying the shower blissfully unaware of its presence. The logical part of his mind tried desperately to soothe the instinctual part that wanted to flee. He knew the spider wouldn't bother him. As his grandfather would have told him, the spider meant him no harm. It found a wet, damp area to hunt for food, and would stay there until hunger or something else forced it to move. Despite this, the potential was there, the potential for something bad to happen, the potential for the spider to fall. That distant possibility of danger made returning to normal and enjoying the shower impossible.

He knew he should deal with the spider. If he didn't deal with it, he'd find webs in more rooms. It would bring more spiders into the apartment. It would procreate, make babies, hundreds of little spiders roaming. He'd find them in his bedroom, in his bed sheets.

He thought about looking for a cup from the kitchen into which to coax the spider. Once caught, he could let it outside. Yes, that seemed like a good idea. Still, he couldn't take his eyes from the spider, fearful that as soon as he looked away the spider would use that moment of vulnerability to leap. What was it about finding bugs inside the home that was so jarring and unsettling? Was it because bugs were a break in the illusion of safety, a reminder that people didn't own the Earth, that we weren't nearly as in control as we thought?

He changed his mind about letting it outside. He should squish it with the shampoo bottle. When people found bugs in their homes, they killed them. That's just how it went.

But still something stopped him. Something buried deep in his mind that empathized with the spider. In a way, the spider seemed more than just a spider. It didn't mean him any harm, hadn't yet shown any indication that it intended harm. It was looking for a place to hunt and to live, that's all.

If Gwen and the child were still living there he'd handle it. But they weren't there, would never be there again. Now it was only him, alone in a two bedroom apartment. No one would care if he let the spider stay. Who was Erik to take away the spider's home? Let it sit there, observe, and eat bugs.

Erik shifted his body and small water droplets splashed up and onto the web. The spider carefully crawled to a dry area of its neat threads. *The itsy-bitsy spider climbed up the shower wall.* Erik sang in his head. *Up splashed the water and washed the spider down.*

He knew that if the steam from the shower continued to lubricate the web, the spider could fall. He could see it clearly in his mind, the spider falling into his hair, down his back, around his ankles, catching on the grate of the drain. The spider, desperately skittering, would then find his toes. Tiny legs would grip that crease between nail and flesh before starting to crawl back up by way of his legs.

He turned off the water, clean enough for now. He kept his eyes on the spider as he stepped out.

As he dressed in his bedroom, he thought about the end of that children's song, about how the spider, even after it fell, kept climbing back up the water spout.

2

Once in bed he tried sleeping on his back but instead found himself staring at the ceiling. He rolled to his side. He was like this for about twenty-five minutes, which he knew because he was staring at the bright digital clock on the end table. He could feel his legs itching to get up and move around. He was thinking about snack food.

He tried to clear his mind. It was past two in the morning, and if he pushed it too far, he'd be stuck in a cycle of staying up to watch the sunrise and sleeping in long after most of the day had already passed. He couldn't do that. He wanted to see the sun, wanted to fix his sleep schedule. It had become irreparably messed up since Gwen and the child had left.

He closed his eyes as they entered his thoughts. Gwen had made her choice. They no longer mattered, no longer existed in his world. It was only him now.

He heard an unbearable hissing in his left ear, like painful television static. He imagined that the hissing was wind blowing against his bedroom window. He closed his eyes and pictured it, the hissing rustling the siding of the apartment during an otherwise quiet night, white noise that would help him sleep.

In reality, his ear drum was broken, shattered from when he was younger and fell asleep with earbuds in, loud music blaring an onslaught of damage. Reality was always much less interesting than the imagination.

After a couple more hours of rolling around in bed, exhaustion and boredom finally took him.

3

Erik awoke just after noon.

"Fuck," he said to no one after seeing the time and realizing he'd slept in. His sleep cycle would continue to slip. At least for the next few days he wouldn't have to really deal with it, he figured. He had the next three days off work.

He got up, not bothering to get dressed, another perk of living alone. In the kitchen he made a grilled cheese sandwich, using a small griddle on the kitchen counter instead of a pan and the stove. The griddle could be wiped clean, whereas the pan would mean a dish that would need to be washed. He cleaned up after he was done, making sure the kitchen remained pristine, no crumbs on the counter. He hated clutter and mess.

He considered eating at the table in the kitchen, as a normal person should, as he'd done with Gwen and the child, but he took his plate with him into the living room instead. He sat on the couch, Gwen's couch, and propped himself up with Gwen's cream-colored pillows. He flipped through movies and television shows to stream before picking a drama that seemed somewhat interesting. Halfway through the movie, he slipped into a nap.

When he awoke, it was late in the afternoon, the dark orange light of another passing day peeking through the blinds of the window behind the television.

"God damn it," he said. He felt heavy and disappointed, watching another day come to an end.

4

That night, as he took his shower, he watched the spider. It seemed as though the spider's web had gotten thicker, and Erik thought the spider might be getting bigger, too. He determined it to be all in his mind. It had to be.

Even if the spider was bigger, he felt at least assured that the spider would not fall, as it was still in the same spot as the night before. He worked shampoo through his hair, eyes closed. When that was done, he bent down to soap and scrub his body. He stood, washed off the soap, and began soaking under the stream of hot water.

In these moments, soaking, he felt serene. He listened to the water landing on his skin, feeling the warmth of the water wrap him into a peaceful cocoon. The act would often add fifteen minutes to each shower, but it was necessary. It helped calm his mind, relaxed him. The outside world, full of toxins, were momentarily kept at bay. The heat of the water burned away the stench of the world.

He sometimes wished he could live the rest of his life in the shower. When Gwen was still living with him, she'd get mad at him for disappearing on her. "Get in and get out," she'd say, "Rub your body with soap and rinse it off. There's no reason to be in there for that long. I don't get it." No, he thought, she didn't get it. She didn't understand how important this was for him. It reset him. Helped him find his neutral.

Erik was so deep in his thoughts, eyes still closed, that he lost his balance and fell forward. The tub was small, the shower head low, and Erik was tall. As he fell forward, his forehead tapped the shower head painfully. He cursed and rubbed his forehead. He felt a sudden surge of adrenaline and irritation, wanting to snap off the shower head. It was thin metal and he could probably break it easily. What stopped him was knowing he'd have to call the landlord and come up with a lie for the mess.

As he stared up at the shower head, his eyes again landed on the spider. A funny memory popped into his mind, as random memories sometimes do. He'd had a teacher once that played an activity with the class. "Raise your hand as high as you can," the teacher had said, and all the students did, stretching them enthusiastically into the air. "Now raise your hand even higher than that," and they all did, raising their hands just a little higher than they had before. The teacher asked, "Why didn't you reach that high the first time?" And everyone looked around shocked, as if he'd played a mind trick on them. At the time it was an inspirational message, that anyone could push themselves to unexpected heights with the right motivation. Erik instead found it to be another bullshit self-lie that inevitably led to disappointment.

The memory became a repeating sound byte in his mind. *Raise your hand as high as you can*, he thought, *now raise it higher still*. He found it to be a strong desire in that moment, to raise his hand up to the spider, to touch it. Then he was doing it, raising his right hand as high as he could, getting it closer and closer to the spider. *Now raise it higher still*, he thought, and did. He stretched his forearm muscles, then stood on the tips of his toes. His fingers were nearly brushing the spider, but not quite there. He could imagine how the bristles would feel when they finally connected.

The spider was inches from his hand now, could leap onto his forefinger if it wanted. It trusted Erik and Erik trusted it.

Unable to reach high enough to fully touch it, he had to drop his hand and reposition his body. He pulled himself up using the curtain rod and stood on the sides of the tub. He did this carefully, making sure the wet plastic would hold his weight. He had a brief image of himself falling, either landing with one leg in the tub, another on the floor, or missing the tub altogether and landing painfully on his ass. It would be fitting to happen to him, he thought. Some people were clutch, making critical moves at the exact right moment. Erik had the opposite instinct, often making the worst possible choice at each juncture. Erik was a habitual failure.

He felt a sturdy hold on the sides of the tub and looked up again. The spider was inches from his head now and he could see it better. The spider's eight legs were spread out evenly like thin fingers. Each leg arched out and bent sharply at two joints, a small claw at the end somehow latching tightly onto the delicate threads of the web. The big blob of a body seemed to be transparent, outside of a long black stripe that didn't quite cover its entire length. Each pulse of its heart seemed to send blood rippling through its skin. The thing was beautiful in its creepy, unreal way. It was designed for a purpose and it did its purpose well.

He was inches away from the spider, the water blast hitting his chest hard, the metal shower head hot against his skin. The spider sat dreadfully still, as if dead. He hoped it wasn't. He made contact with it.

The spider shifted and scurried into its hole in the ceiling tile, disappearing from sight.

The movement startled Erik and he fell back, instinctively thinking the spider had leapt at him. He slapped at his skin, nerves firing as he swatted the non-existent spider off his body. He slipped and flailed his arms, hoping to grab something as he fell back. He managed to grip the thin plastic of the shower curtain and held himself suspended in the air, trying to regain balance. For a second the plastic curtain held him, and he stood there, muscles flexed. Time froze as he desperately, slowly, tried to pull himself back up onto his feet. Clap, the first plastic clip holding up the curtain broke. The rest quickly followed. *Clap clap clapclapclap*. He fell through the air and landed on the ceramic floor. His neck hit the rim of the toilet and he felt electricity jolt through his neck, back, and elbows.

He sat there for a moment, absorbing the moment. This was precisely something Erik would do. Some people came in clutch, but never Erik. Erik was anti-clutch.

His ass was cold against the tile of the floor, his neck in pain, but he didn't feel like moving yet. He felt embarrassed at first, but the anger came as it always did. The water hit his knees, dripped down, and pooled on the floor around him, instantly becoming ice cold. It felt good on his raw elbows, but his testicles were painfully frigid. He looked up at the corner where the spider had been, but couldn't see it. Fucking spider. He thought. He felt oddly betrayed.

He sighed, lifted one arm, and rubbed his neck. He tried to get up but the edges of the tub cut into the undersides of his knees and he dropped back down once pain shot through his legs. On the second attempt he went a little slower. Once upright he turned off the water. He grabbed a towel and threw it on the wet floor. He dried his face with another. He looked up at the corner above the shower head again. Still no spider. Only a web saturated with water droplets.

So the spider was gone. He figured things would go back to normal now without the excitement of the spider. But what was normal, exactly? Staying up late watching television and sleeping through the day? Leaving the house only to work, then come home?

Normal was pointless. Meaningless.

He was surprised to find that he missed Gwen, the child, and the uncertainty they added to his life. Sure, his apartment was clean and organized and exactly how he wanted it, down to the perfect heat setting and the placement of the furniture. Sometimes, though, he missed coming home to shoes being in a pile, not put away. The television being left on with no one watching it. The dishes piling up in the sink. Snack wrappers scattered on the floor. Toys in the middle of the floor for him to trip on. That chaos brought life into the home. Made it home. Whatever it was that he had now was not a home. It was barely life.

Life needed.... *Life*.

He hit the wall in front of him with a closed fist. Softly at first. Testing out how it felt. The impact was a soft thud, but still felt firm against his knuckles. It numbed his fingers. He hit the wall again, a little harder, then again and again, each time with a little more force. He hit until he saw blood on his knuckles and they started to feel raw.

He stopped, enjoying the pain pumping up his arm, the feeling of raw energy, a mimicry of living, the release. Then he felt shame as he looked at the dented sheetrock in the wall. He'd have to repair it before the landlord saw it. He washed his knuckles under warm water, rubbing them softly until the pain went away.

5

Still naked, he stepped into the living room. He was thinking he should go to bed, but because he'd taken a nap, he wasn't feeling tired enough for that. He looked at the couch but couldn't stomach sitting there to watch any more television. He wandered into the kitchen, looked around, then stepped into the spare room.

It was once the child's room, but had since become a storage room. He remembered seeing Gwen in there, that last time.

"I'll come back for our stuff," Gwen had said, "When we find a place."

"Just stay until you have another place, Gwen."

She'd said nothing, only looked at him, holding the child close. A mama bear protecting her cub. She'd seemed to be considering her words, her lips moving a few times, but she didn't say anything at all.

"So I have to watch your stuff for you, then?" Erik had said to break the awkward silence, tired of waiting.

She'd backed toward the door, irritating him more.

"I can pay you if you want," she'd said, "It won't be for long. I'm staying with a friend for now until I can save up for a deposit."

He'd felt used. She had a way of making him feel used. There had been pressure bubbling up in his forehead and he'd wanted to release it but didn't know how. He wanted her to pay for what she was doing to him, wanted to extend the internal tension that he was feeling to her, because it was only fair. He wanted to yell, to scream until the pressure eased. But he didn't. The image of the child hiding behind her mother had stopped him. A child scared of a monster.

Their stuff was still in that room, still waiting to be picked up. He'd since packed everything into boxes, preparing for the day where it would leave his possession. The boxes were stacked neatly against the back wall. It was all there in front of him, their stuff, their memories, locked behind a wall of cardboard. Reminders of things better left forgotten. He could faintly smell them in the room, their essence hovering like ghosts, seeping out from the closed flaps of the boxes.

He didn't like going into the room and wasn't sure why he'd wandered into the room in the first place. Perhaps the incident in the bathroom was making him feel off. He never really understood his own emotions, didn't know why he did the things he did. He felt things, and those feelings made him do things, and that was all. He stepped up to the wall of boxes and sat down on the carpet in front of them as if the boxes were cardboard shrines. The box closest to him was a rather large box, which he knew specifically held some of Gwen's clothing. His heart raced as he sat there, a person tending to their faith after years of absence, ready to ask for forgiveness.

He knew he shouldn't do it, but he knew that he would. He had nothing else to do to kill the time. Gwen hadn't called to ask about the stuff since she'd left, and all this stuff was garbage waiting to be thrown out. The flaps of the box were bent in such a way that he could see glimpses of her clothing inside. He opened the box.

On top was a faded blue sweater. He remembered it right away. It was Gwen's late night wear, her *it's almost bedtime and I'm lazy* sweater. She'd worn it nearly every night and rarely washed it, putting it on when the day was late and lazily tossing it onto the dresser when it was time for bed. He picked up the sweater and pressed it to his face, inhaling her faint smell. He pretended that the pressure he placed on the back side of the sweater was her body. He pretended he was cuddled up to her on the couch, resting his head just below her breasts where he could listen to her breathe.

He passed out in the room with the sweater wrapped around his face.

6

His ringing phone woke him. Daylight shone in through the blinds. It was morning. He found the phone in the living room. It was cold against his cheek as he answered it.

"Hello?"

"Hey, Erik? You okay? Haven't heard from you," the voice said.

"Yeah, fine, Cam. I haven't heard from you, either," Erik said.

"The guys and I were talking that we haven't gotten together in awhile."

There was silence after the statement. Erik knew his friend Cameron had asked an indirect question. It annoyed him. Cameron was asking Erik to do the work for him, to suggest that they get together, to make plans that Erik had no interest in. Why did people do that? He thought the world would be a better place if people would speak their intent instead of waiting for others to figure out what they wanted. Gwen did it, too. The only difference was that Erik would often misread what she'd want, or would miss that she'd wanted anything at all.

Erik said nothing, letting the silence linger, refusing to let his friend get away with his bullshit.

"You there?"

"Yeah."

"You good?"

"Yeah I'm fine, Cam. Just woke up. A little out of it. What's up?"

"So what are you doing tonight?"

"Not sure. Just hanging out at home probably."

"Want to hang with me and the guys?"

Erik considered. He didn't, but he also wanted to leave the house. He knew he needed to see people, thought often about getting out and doing something. But whenever he did plan to get out, he realized how much he didn't want to see anyone after all.

"Where?" He asked.

"My place. Probably play a board game. Get pizza."

It sounded nice, but also exhausting. Either way, he needed to get out.

"Yeah, I'd be up for that." He said.

"Great. We're thinking six or so?"

"Alright, I'll be over around then."

"Great. It'll be nice to catch up."

"Yeah."

"You sure you're good? Need a lift tonight?"

"No. I'll be fine."

"Okay. See you then."

"See you."

The line went dead. Erik dropped the phone from his ear and stared at the background. It was still a photo of Gwen, him, and the child. In the photo, the child was a small baby between them. The picture had been set on his phone by Gwen a long time ago and never changed. Why hadn't he changed the picture yet? Laziness? Probably not. Like everything else, deep down in his gut, he knew there was something he didn't want to deal with yet, and deleting that picture was part of it. Dealing with it meant accepting, acknowledging what he'd done. It was easier to pretend that this was all Gwen's fault, or the child's fault, because this shitty loneliness could *not* be on him.

He closed his fist around his phone and squeezed as hard as he could, wanting the screen to crack in his grip. He wanted to feel glass shards from the screen pierce his flesh. The thought of blood on the ground, around his torn skin, an open wound down to bone, felt exhilarating. The phone was stubborn and wouldn't break so he threw it at the wall instead. It hit with a thud and fell with a smack against the floor tiling, bouncing a couple times before landing screen-up. The screen lit up. Erik could see a crack running through the on screen family like a fissure.

Going into the room had been a mistake. He couldn't trust his feelings. He wouldn't go in there again.

7

Later that day, Erik was bored and trying to pass time until he saw his friends. He went into the bathroom to look for the spider. As he stood outside the tub, looking up into the corner of the walls where it had been, he couldn't find it on its web.

He stared up at the web, waiting for the spider to appear, hands in the pockets of his sweatpants. Perhaps it was hiding somewhere in the ceiling, or maybe it had moved along the ceiling tile into one of the side rooms. All that was left of it now was its disjointed, messy web.

He remembered reading somewhere that spiders didn't make new web, that they only had what they were born with. He was certain that this was bullshit and figured they grew web like humans grew hair. If it was true, though, then the spider had gone and left its home behind. Now the web was just another mess to clean up. It no longer looked clean and purposeful. Strands were broken from the chaos of the night before, gaping holes scattered around its design.

He considered going to get a broom, but decided he didn't need a broom to clean up this mess. As he had done the night before, he stepped onto the sides of the tub. This time he made sure to have a solid hold, one hand gripping the shower pole firmly. The tub was dry and less slippery, which also helped. With his free hand extended, he swirled his pointer finger around the web as if it were cotton candy.

Before he'd gotten a third of the web cleared, the spider crawled out from the hole in the ceiling and onto his finger. It didn't stop. Its legs felt similar to that of a fly as it ran up his hand, then his arm. Erik could barely follow it's fast trek with his eyes. In a panicked state he shook his arm, hoping to fling the spider from him. The fat thing, which was significantly larger now than it had been the first night he saw it, held firm, continuing its race up his arm and into his shirt sleeve. He could feel it scratching in there as it ran across his chest.

Erik leapt out of the tub. He shook himself vigorously, patting at his chest, arms, and then his face. He took his shirt off, looking inside and outside of it then up and down his body. He couldn't find the spider. He searched the floor and the walls in the bathroom, but still it was nowhere to be seen.

He left the bathroom. He checked himself again in the living room. He could feel it, its furry legs racing up his arm and across its chest, even though he couldn't see it. He took a deep breath to relax his nerves.

He checked the time on his phone. There were a few more hours to pass until it was time to head to Cameron's. Still feeling rattled, he sat on the couch to watch television, content to sit and do nothing. He felt things crawling on his skin as he watched, but there was never anything there.

8

Sometime later the television images began swirling together. Erik had long stopped caring what the images meant. He didn't really watch television for stories, but instead for the energy, the mock movement.

In his peripheral he noticed that the living room didn't seem quite right. He stood to get a better view of the place and found the problem. The couch seemed to be in the wrong spot. He tried pulling it back to the center of the room, where it was supposed to be, at just the right distance from the television, but as he heaved he found that he couldn't make progress. He wasn't strong enough to make the room as it should be. His body felt like rubber. He decided to move around to the other side to push it back into place instead.

When he turned, he saw the spider. It was much larger now, impossibly large, nearly half Erik's height. It stood on four of its fragmented back legs like a minotaur. Its body was covered in dark brown, needle-like fur and its abdomen was shifted down in such a way that Erik could see its many black, beady eyes, glistening in the light of the room. The other four legs bent and snapped in the air slowly, threateningly. Its fangs twitched hungrily alongside the mandible-like arms attached to its head. Spit dripped from its mouth.

Curiously, the thought in Erik's mind wasn't about how the spider had grown so large, but instead about why insects always looked so wet. After this thought, which he didn't conclude with any personal theory, he wondered how long it had been since the spider ate. He'd destroyed its web, after all.

Was any of this even real? Was he going crazy? Had his mind finally snapped? How could he know for sure? When a person was all alone, who was there to challenge their perspective, to confirm what was real or imagined?

As they stared at each other, man and spider, Erik realized with horror that he'd sized things up all wrong. Different species could never coexist together. The spider wasn't peaceful. Back when it was small, its size had been deceptive. Now they were approaching an equal size, and the danger was visible for what it truly was.

He picked up a pillow from the couch, one of Gwen's pillows, and the spider watched him. Its four suspended arms hovered in the air, alert but not threatened. He flicked the pillow at the spider, intending to distract it. The spider caught the pillow with three of its arms with ease. Its head tilted as it examined the object, and seconds passed uneventfully. Erik backed away toward the door, intending to flee the apartment.

As his hand graced the doorknob, his gateway to freedom, the spider began doing a curious thing. It spun the pillow. It used two of its suspended legs as an axle as a third pushed to give it momentum. When the pillow was spinning at its fastest, the fourth arm grabbed a loose thread as it whipped around. The pillow began to unravel. A pile of thread pooled on the ground. White stuffing once trapped inside the pillow was flung across the room in chunks. The task took no more than a minute to complete.

With the pillow disintegrated, the spider turned around. The apartment seemed to shake as it did, its furry, fragmented legs lifting and snapping, lifting and snapping, mechanically stabbing into the floor with each step. When the back of the spider was facing Erik, he saw a hole back there, and Erik instinctively knew the hole to be the place where the web was released. The spider began absorbing the pile of thread on the floor, sucking it up like water from a straw.

Once the thread had been absorbed, the spider moved toward the spare room. It must have grown even more, because Erik noticed its head nearly touched the top of the door frame. It had to squeeze its wide body through the doorway to get into the room.

Erik approached the room. Where the spider's body had squished through there remained a sticky clear liquid dripping from the frame. He stared inside. He found it too dark to see the spider. He could hear it scratching as it moved around in the darkness. There was a flash of many white lights in the back corner of the room, and Erik realized that they were its eyes.

Erik closed the door.

9

He awoke on the floor of the kitchen. His back and elbows hurt. He could hear the television on in the living room, and then realized that he had fallen asleep. Did he sleep walk into the kitchen? He didn't recall ever sleep walking before, but everything had to start somewhere.

Parts of what must have been the dream came back to him, and he looked at the door to the spare room, remembering the spider's eyes looking back at him from within the darkness. The door remained shut.

He remembered his plans for the night and looked out the kitchen window. It was late into the night, no light shining through. He slipped his phone from his pocket to check the time. One in the morning, long past time to meet with his friends. He had several texts and missed calls from Cameron.

As a wave of disappointment fell over him, he thought about killing himself. The thought came unexpectedly, but was nothing more than a passing thought. It was a fantasy for finding a sense of permanent peace. He knew he wouldn't do it, but it was an intense thought regardless.

He stood and turned out the lights. He walked to his bedroom. He undressed and slipped into bed. He laid there, listened to the scratching in his ear, not feeling tired. His mind was empty. Everything felt empty. He didn't want to lie there, but there was nothing else to d o.

He fell asleep when the sky outside finished its transition from black to purple to red to orange.

10

When he awoke, he texted Cam to apologize for missing his calls, explaining that he'd fallen asleep. He waited for a response but it never came.

He decided to call Gwen. He needed a reason to call her and decided he'd ask her when she planned to pick up her stuff. He looked up her name and number in his phone, which he hadn't yet deleted. As her name flashed across the screen, he paused to stare at it for a long while.

He knew it was a bad idea to call her, just as it had been a bad idea to enter the spare room, but he wanted to hear her voice. He was upset about the previous night and needed a win. Would calling Gwen make him feel the way he desperately wanted to feel? His thumb hovered over the call button. His chest hurt. He felt like a child in high school calling his crush for the first time. Why was this so hard? Why was everything so hard? He squeezed the phone in frustration, wanting to break it.

He took a deep breath and released. Why was he so angry all the time? He thought about getting help, something Gwen had frequently suggested. Maybe a therapist would help him talk through whatever the fuck was going on in his head.

Inevitably he kicked that thought aside as he always did. What would a therapist tell him that he didn't already know? He knew he was angry. He considered himself smarter than the average person. Less-than-average people needed therapists, people that needed real help, people that couldn't help themselves. Not him. Talking to someone about how he was feeling would be a waste of time. He could fix himself because he knew what was going on. He just needed to keep everything under control.

He heard a scratching sound in the spare room and looked over at the door. The sound was quiet, barely there, deep into the room behind the closed door. It could have been his fucked up ear, but he felt that it was something more. He approached the door, just to check. The noises increased as he got closer. Something was definitely moving around in there.

With his mind distracted, his thumb graced the green dial button on the phone. He heard the dial tone begin and had a momentary panic attack. He quickly put the phone to his ear. Then he lowered it again, finger hovering over the end call button. He didn't know what to do, what he wanted to do. What would he say if she answered? He reminded himself of the stuff she needed to come pick up, and found it to be a decent excuse. Was the spider in there now, destroying those things she might one day come back for?

He returned the phone to his ear and held his breath. Two more rings passed, then three, then four. She wouldn't answer, he thought. He dropped the phone again to hang up.

"Erik?" Came a quiet voice from the phone. Gwen's voice.

He felt butterflies in his chest at the sound. He raised the phone back to his ear.

"Hello? Erik, are you there?"

Her voice. It had been so long. He felt everything in his core surge at her sound, like nothing else mattered but that voice. He'd do anything for this woman, if she'd give him the chance. He'd be a better man. He'd manage his temper. He'd be patient. He'd be decent. He'd keep himself under control. He'd go talk to a therapist, if she still wanted t hat.

"Are you there? Did you mean to call?" the voice asked.

"Gwen," he said, forgetting what his excuse was. "Gwen, can I see you? I want to see you."

"Oh, I don't... I don't think that's a good idea."

Reality returned. This wasn't a dream world. The image of the child crying returned to him and he wanted to scream, to forget. He was a monster. A dangerous man. Seemingly harmless on the surface, but something dark was inside him.

"Oh, no, not like that," he said, "I mean, just to get your stuff."

A long pause. "I think you should just throw all of it," she said.

He had expected this, in a way, but hearing it, that the stuff meant nothing to her, still had an impact. It confirmed that she'd never be coming back.

"Erik? I think I should hang up."

"Gwen, no. What do you mean throw it? It's fine, I packed it all up in boxes for you."

"Erik, stop."

"What?"

"It's been weeks, and this is the first time you've called. This is what you want to talk about?"

"What do you mean?"

"You're not going to ask about Audrey?"

The child. No, he didn't want to talk about the child.

"You're not going to ask how she's doing? How heartless are you?"

Yes, heartless. A heartless monster. The spider was the perfect roommate, his true soul mate. He didn't deserve anyone but the spider. He shouldn't have called.

"I hope silence is your regret, asshole."

The line went dead. He sat there stupidly with the phone to his ear for a long time, unsure of what to do next.

Was he supposed to work today? He couldn't remember what day it was. Every action was done only to pass the time. Eat, sleep, shower, repeat. This was life now. No, not life. Survival.

He figured it didn't matter if he worked. If he was fired, so be it. He'd sit in this apartment alone until the day he died.

He turned on the television.

11

"Daddy, drink?" the child asks.

"No, go, I have a headache," daddy says.

He sits on the couch watching television. He's tired and feeling lazy. He wants to sit and exist for a moment after coming home from work but he can't because mommy works the night shift. This is the way it has to be because there's no money left for day care. Before the child, mommy and daddy worked the same hours and kept the afternoons for themselves. Mommy would do her things, daddy would do his. Now daddy has to work during the day shift and be a babysitter at night, questioning why he did this to himself. He's never wanted to be a father, but now he is trapped, and the world around him is too busy, too noisy. The child is more noise, and with it around he can't find peace. Life is like a television show with interference, lines of static shooting across the screen and muddying up the story. Static, hissing, static, hissing. He can't focus. Doesn't it understand that daddy needs time alone? Daddy needs a reset.

"Daddy, drink," the child says, thrusting an empty bottle in daddy's face.

"Audrey, go away," daddy says. The child can be thirsty for a fucking minute. Just a minute, that's all he's asking for. It needs to leave him alone.

Instead, it's back in seconds. "Daddy, drink!" it says.

"Fuck off," he says. He grabs the cup and throws it.

The plastic cup clacks against the wall before bouncing to the floor. The child's lips pucker in a pout that irritates him more. Put that fucking lip away, he thinks. He wants just a few more minutes to watch television and be left alone. Just half an hour, then he can go be a father.

But the fucking child.

It walks away, then comes back, cup in hand. He thinks about getting up and getting it water, just to satisfy it, but he feels so tired. Everything is exhausting, every action.

"Daddy. I. Thirsty!" It says, and throws the cup with precision at daddy's face. It hits him in the eye. He knows it wasn't intentional, but it doesn't matter. It hurts. It hurts and he must react.

"God dammit, Audrey!" He screams.

Such a stupid name, mommy's choice. Such a stupid child. He stands up, a big man towering over a small child, the cup in his hand. The child is crying, scared. This makes daddy happy. It should be scared. But the crying is more static, more lines on the television, and it all needs to stop. "Shut up," he screams at the child, "Stop fucking crying." But the little thing doesn't stop. Instead the crying gets louder. It doesn't know what to do. It hasn't learned to think about other people's wants yet, only its own. It's a selfish thing.

He knows what needs to happen to stop it from crying. He needs to give it a bottle, and now he will need to hold it and reassure it to calm it down, too. He doesn't want to do any of it. He wants the child to learn obedience and respect. His head is throbbing, both from the hit to his eye, the adrenaline, and the lingering headache from work. He doesn't want to appease this stupid little thing. It's all hissing and static in his ears.

"Shut up, there's nothing to fucking cry about," he says, and the crying becomes wailing.

The child is cowering from him now, holding its little hands up, like he's a monster. He's not a monster, he just needs to be alone for a minute.

"Stop, I'll get you water, just stop crying."

The crying is so loud, ringing in his ears. The pain in his head is worse, from the hit or from the adrenaline he doesn't know. He turns to walk to the kitchen, but the child is still wailing, screaming. It doesn't realize that it's won, the selfish little thing. The child will grow up spoiled, getting everything it wants, feeding off of him like a parasite. One parasite of many, all feeding off of daddy, and he wants to rid himself of the toxins and be free and be alone and be at fucking peace. The child's screams are echoing now, back and forth, back and forth, from one side of his skull to the next.

"Fucking, shut up!" he screams, turns, and throws.

The reaction is one of emotion, consciousness overridden by the need to react. For a second, he is a creature directed uncontrollably by his anger. He thinks he can control those angry thoughts, keep them buried, still make rational decisions despite them, but when given the opportunity to entertain them his subconscious gladly does. Without realizing it, he's been fostering a bomb. Don't think, act, and ask for forgiveness later.

He means to throw the cup at the ground, to scare the child so it stops crying. At least this is what he tells himself, as the cup hits the child in the head. An eye for an eye, as they say. The child, surprised, recoils and falls backward. Its head bounces on the floor. The crying stops and the child lays there, stunned, its eye swelling. It lifts itself from the floor in shock. They stare at each other for awhile.

The child vomits.

Daddy calls mommy for help.

When mommy gets there, she leaves the apartment with the child.

Daddy goes and sits on the couch and watches television, welcoming the silence and time alone.

It's finally quiet.

No more static.

No more hissing.

For now.

12

A knock at the door woke Erik from his nap. Orange light passed through the shades of the window next to the door. Three more knocks follow.

"Erik, you in there?" Comes a muffled voice from outside.

He could see a person hold a hand up to the window, trying to peer through the blinds. Erik stood and went to the door. He opened it and was blinded by light. Once his eyes adjusted, he saw Cameron. It was quiet, the morning cool. The air tasted clean and he breathed it in deeply.

"Hey," Cameron said, "You alright, man?"

"Yeah, I'm fine, why?" Erik asked.

Cameron didn't respond at first, seemed to be inspecting him, which made him feel uncomfortable. Did he look that out of place? He wanted to go back inside and hide. It was too bright out here.

"Do you want to go inside and talk?" Cameron asked.

He looked inside, at the door to the spare room, the spider still inside scratching away, the sound howling in his ear. Could Cameron hear it? He stepped outside and shut the door.

"No, out here is fine."

"Okay."

There was a quiet pause, both waiting for the other to make the first move. Cameron had come here without a plan, a wellness check. Cameron was no friend. Cameron was someone who didn't want to feel guilty when something bad happened. Cameron wanted to be able to tell people he'd done everything he could.

"I've been trying to get a hold of you, but your phone must be dead," Cameron said.

Erik took his phone out of his pocket. The battery was dead. He remembered talking to Gwen on the phone. How long ago was that? He thought it had been earlier that day. Trying to remember the passage of time made him feel sick. He wanted to go back to bed.

"I forgot to charge my phone last night. I've been busy." He put the phone in his pocket.

"Doing what?"

"Just busy. Taking care of stuff."

"Something in your apartment? It looks like you haven't left in a while."

"How would you know that?"

"Just the way you look, man."

"How do I look?"

He was getting irritated again. He needed this to end. He needed to be left alone. He needed to go back inside and disappear into a cocoon of sheets and block out the light.

"You look... drained. Like something is eating at you. I can't imagine what it's been like since they left, but-"

"I'm fine, why are you here?" He interrupted.

He saw a hole in the concrete below him and kicked dirt into it. As soon as he did, small black ants began digging their way out. He kicked the dirt back in as they climbed, grinding the ants into the concrete.

"I'm worried about you, man."

"Because of Gwen? The child?"

Cameron was quiet for a moment, considering his words. "What happened was fucked up, Erik. But it was an accident."

The ants were swarming now. He'd started something he couldn't stop. There were too many. They kept coming, crawling onto his feet. He started stomping on them. He could feel Cameron's eyes on him.

"Want to do something tonight?" Cameron asked.

"Not really."

"Really, I think you need a break."

"Fuck off, I'm fine," he said.

"When's the last time you were around people?"

"I don't need people. I keep myself company."

Erik was stomping, killing the ants that kept coming, twisting his foot with to make sure they were dead. Were they slowing down, or was that in his head, too?

"What are you doing, Erik?"

Erik looked up. Cameron was looking at him like he'd lost his mind. Maybe he had.

"Please leave, Cam," he said and stepped back inside, shutting and locking the door behind him.

Erik watched Cameron's shadow pace back and forth in front of the door for a few minutes before leaving.

13

The scratching in the spare room was becoming unbearably loud, so much so that he couldn't hear anything else. He wondered if his neighbors heard it. He tried plugging his ears with his fingers, but the volume didn't relent. It rattled in his head, the never-ending scratching, the hissing. Erik had to stop it. He went to the spare room and opened the door. He looked at the changed room in shock, as the kitchen light filtered in.

The cardboard boxes where Gwen's and the child's things had once been stored were broken down and shredded. The spider had a new web, using the clothing inside the boxes like it had the pillow, and the web was a rainbow of different colors spread out over the back half of the room. He looked around the web for the soft blue of the worn sweater he loved, hoping it was still whole, but there were so many colors he couldn't see where it might have been. He felt tears in his eyes at the loss. Gwen and the child were fully gone, all aspects, all memories, gone.

Yet, maybe not. He stepped into the room and approached the web. He noticed that each section had different thicknesses due to the variety of materials used. He could see rough cotton threads and rougher areas where denim had been used. There was a silky, lacy thread that he recognized as Gwen's panties, most of them shiny and vibrant against the rest of the dull material.

By staring at the threads, he found himself remembering what she looked like in each different pair, her belly button just above them, the way she pulled her feet through as she stepped out of them. He leaned as close to the threads as he dared, wanting to lay upon them. He wanted to smell her, to feel something that had once touched her. He graced the top of one section of the thread with his hand and saw an image of her in a tank top, her nipples poking through her shirt. He touched another and could see her in a sweatshirt, lying on the couch and eating potato chips. He hated the kind she liked because they made her breath stink, but it was a part of her all the same. He touched another thread and saw her in the t-shirt she'd worn when they'd first met, wondering what it would be like to kiss her again. He touched another thread and saw her in her bathrobe, straightening her hair, catching him looking and giving him a look that said, "quit being weird". He laid his head down against the web and yes, he could smell her again. Not her perfume, but her skin, her particular kind of sweat, and he was relieved. She wasn't completely gone. She was preserved in the thread.

Then he touched a thread that wasn't Gwen at all. It took him some time, but it became clear. It was the thread of a stuffed bear. The child's bear. The bear that had been a gift from grandma when the child was born, purchased from the hospital's gift shop. When the child started talking and understanding, it had taken the bear with it everywhere, its prized possession. How had the bear been left behind? Did Gwen and the child really leave so quickly, so afraid of him, so afraid of the monster, that the child's favorite toy was left behind? Now it was shredded, a tool for the spider, the monster, the destroyer of homes. He hated the spider.

He could feel the threads of the web moving and knew the spider was coming. He looked up and was staring into its eyes, each one large enough now that he saw his own reflection staring back inside of them. The spider's face was fuzzy, the skin of a spoiled peach, and he saw the wetness dripping from its fangs so close to his own face.

Erik released the web hesitatingly, not wanting to leave those memories behind to this disgusting thing, but knew he had no choice. He turned toward the door to run. He was at the opening when he felt a bony appendage grab at one of his legs, sandpaper against his skin. The spider tried to pull him back into the room and onto the web, but Erik fought, pulling himself out of the door with the thing still grasping his leg. Erik strained, pulled with all his strength, desperate to escape the threshold. The spider was strong, but Erik proved stronger. He pulled the leg through the door frame and slammed the door.

As the door closed, there was a wet squealing sound coming from inside. A split appendage was lying on the ground by the door, twitching. He kicked the leg into a corner of the kitchen and out of sight. The spider was continuing to get bigger, he realized, was still growing. How long before it outgrew that room, outgrew Erik's ability to contain it?

14

When the lock to the apartment disengaged and Gwen stepped inside, Erik was certain he was hallucinating. She looked at him, sitting on the couch, hands in his pockets, and shut the door as she stepped in. To Erik, Gwen was radiant, a glowing light entering a dark, shameful place.

"Hey," he said.

"Hey," she said.

Gwen seemed to feel as out of place as he felt, both of them not knowing how to navigate their new dynamic. Habit pulled at him like a magnet, and Erik so badly wanted to embrace, to touch her. He felt good in her presence, had forgotten what that felt like.

"What's going on with you?" She asked.

"Nothing, why?"

"Cam texted me, said he stopped by and was worried about you."

"I was just tired."

She was analyzing him. She didn't seem angry or fearful of him like she had when she left, and Erik wondered what had changed. He wondered, but he knew. The child wasn't here. Gwen could stand up to him when she didn't have a child to protect.

"Are you sleeping a lot again?" She asked, "Are you still hitting things?"

"No." He lied.

"Then why is Cam so worried? Jesus, this place is trashed."

He wanted to hug her so bad, to touch her, for things to go back to normal. He felt a tug, a pull toward her that was almost unbearable. He needed her.

"Gwen, can you stay for a bit?" He asked.

She seemed hesitant, but she must have seen something in his eyes.

"Okay, but nothing is happening. We're just going to talk."

"Okay."

She sat on the couch, a safe distance from him.

"What have you been hitting?" She asked.

He looked at his knuckles, still raw from the incident in the bathroom. He felt both pride and shame as he rubbed them. The prideful part of him, the uncontrollable monster, thought that the battle wounds showed his power, his strength. The shameful part, however, knew the truth. The shame understood that he was struggling, knew that the anger was part depression, part broken psyche stretched to its limits. If he went in for help, what would he find to be the origin of all this? Maybe there was no origin at all. Maybe these things just happened.

"Erik, you should go in and ask for help."

He opened his mouth to respond, but she held up a hand.

"I'll tell you why I came, and then we can move on. Just let me talk."

He wanted to say something, to protest, but knew he'd lose her forever if he did. He nodded.

"I'm still mad at you. You need to know that. You hurt Audrey. Gave her a damn concussion."

He could feel pressure building in the back of his mind. She'd come for a fight. After all this time apart, she was back and it was going to be a fight. He was ready. He was always ready for a fight. He no longer cared about mending things.

"I know it was an accident, okay?" She said, and Erik's thoughts melted away, "I see that you're struggling, and I want you to know that it was just an accident. It was a terrible thing that could have ended far worse, but I don't think you're a bad person. I'm so mad at you, but you're not a bad person, Erik. You have things that you need help with, and you need to get help before... Before something worse happens."

She paused, but Erik didn't have anything to say.

"I came because I want you to know that I forgive you. I don't hate you. I'm mad at you, but I don't hate you. Someday, Audrey might forgive you, too. But not for a long time. And not unless you get help. I wanted to come here and help you find closure. I think you might need that right now. We're done, Erik. That part of our lives together is over. But I still care about you, and you're still Audrey's father. I don't want anything bad to happen to you."

Erik wanted to respond, but nothing felt adequate. He was feeling things again, but didn't know what they were or how to handle them. He dropped his head into his hands. He still wanted to die. He'd lost control, and things couldn't go back to how they were. So what could he do? What was he going to do? He felt Gwen stand from the couch.

"Audrey left the bear here and wants it," Gwen said, "Do you remember that thing? The gift from my mom? It's important to her. I'm hoping its here. That's all I need. The rest can be thrown."

From inside the protection of his hands, he could hear Gwen's soft steps on the tile. She was walking toward the spare room, toward Audrey's old room. He jumped up.

"No, don't. Don't go in there," he said, but she was already at the door.

She turned the handle and stepped inside. The spider hissed as light fell into the room.

"What the fuck..." Gwen said.

"Gwen, get out of there!"

Erik was at the door now, saw the spider approaching her. It could smell her, the owner of its web. It craved her, needed her essence. Erik put his arms around Gwen, intent to throw her from the room. Before Erik could pull Gwen from the room, the spider had reached out with two of it's long, segmented legs, legs still whole, and took hold of her. She screamed. Erik pulled at her waist, but the spider pulled as well. It was much stronger now, always getting stronger, bigger, faster. It slashed at her with a third leg and cut her arm. Gwen yelled out as blood dripped down.

"Let go, let go, let go!" she screamed, but the spider refused.

"No," Erik screamed, "No, you can't have her!"

He was losing ground. They were being pulled deeper into the room.

"No, Gwen, I won't let it have you," he said, pulling as hard as he could.

"Erik, what the fuck!" She screamed.

He was lost in the moment, finally holding her again, arms around her waist, in the same hold he'd done so many times before. He could feel the warm blood of her arms falling onto him as he held her. The spider was too big now, too strong. He and Gwen inched toward its mouth together, and he knew he'd have a front row seat to her death. Gwen didn't think he was a monster, but Erik knew he was. His neglect had led to this. He'd let the thing into his home, had let it live and fester. He should have dealt with it earlier. He should have killed it when he first became aware of its presence.

He wept into Gwen's neck as he held her for the last time, as she screamed, the fangs of the spider nearing the vulnerable flesh of her face. That face, which he'd held delicately between his hands when they were still in love, would be ripped from her skull, eyes sucked out like grapes, blood drained as her remains decayed on the web in that spare room. And Erik would... what? Leave the room and let the spider continue to grow until it eventually took him, too? And what of Audrey? Audrey.... Oh, Audrey...

They'd never be a family again. Maybe he was forgivable, but he wouldn't get back what he had. That was gone forever.

He let go of Gwen.

She lurched forward toward the spider, but awkwardly from the force of being let go.

Before the spider could take her into its jaws, Erik leapt forward and jammed his arm as deep as he could down its throat. The fangs tore at the skin of his arm, a thousand sharp jabs into his flesh. His hand inside the mouth was crushed, and he felt as if he were fainting. He pushed through it. He hit the spider with his other hand, slamming his closed fist into the spider's eyes one by one like he were playing whack-a-mole. One eye flattened, and puss shot out from it, caking his face. The spider shrieked, a hideous sound that reminded Erik of a video he saw once of a hawk eating a baby rabbit, the rabbit crying out until it couldn't cry anymore. Erik continued to pound the head of the spider, ignoring the searing pain of what was left of the hand inside the spider's throat.

Finally, the spider relented. It let go of Gwen, stabbing its now two free legs into Erik's back instead. He groaned, felt blood soak into his clothing, felt nauseous and weak. He turned his head, met eyes with Gwen, just before she ran out of the room.

The spider continued to stab him, over and over and over, until he passed out.

15

Erik woke lying on the web. He saw the spider above him, more vividly now as light seeped in from behind the window shades. The spider's many eyes glistened as the sun hit them. He saw with pride that he'd damaged some those eyes. He counted four of them that were nothing more than punctured sacks of dripping jelly. Erik realized that he was no longer being stabbed by the spider, but he still felt sick and numb, as if his body knew that it was dying.

He tried to move, shifted his body as best he could, but couldn't. He glanced down, saw his lower half surrounded by web. The spider was working to wrap him thickly in the web of Gwen and Audrey's clothing. The web vibrated and rocked slowly underneath him as the spider spun it tightly. Soon it was up to his chest, and it was getting harder to breathe. The spider wrapped him, tighter and tighter, thread by thread. He closed his eyes and tried to go to sleep, but sleep did not come. He was enveloped in darkness as the spider covered his head.

The last sound Erik heard, as the spider injected its stomach acid into the cocoon, his casket, was a scratching sound just behind his left ear.

INSIDE A CONCRETE BOX

30

"I believe that what we become depends on what our fathers teach us at odd moments, when they aren't trying to teach us. We are formed by little scraps of wisdom." –Umberto Eco

"Dads are most ordinary men turned by love into heroes, adventurers, story-tellers, and singers of song." –Pam Brown

1

"**D**ad!" she screamed, her lungs propelling the sound as deep into the trees as was possible for her age. There was no response outside the rustling of the dead trees surrounding her. Her face was covered in tears. Where had her father gone? How could he have abandoned her in this place? "Dad, where are you?" She yelled out again, to no avail.

Her little brother was beside her, crying more profusely than she. Snot dribbled from his nose. He held onto her arm tightly, following her wherever she went, nearly dragging her to the ground. She ran as fast as she could, dragging him along through the trees, seeking escape. She didn't know which direction would lead them to freedom. Everything looked the same, an endless sea of towering wood pillars. Her arms and legs were leaking red from scratches, trees attempting to slow her down as best they could. The wind endlessly howled. It cut through the tall trees above her, branches bending and creaking, the only sounds in the night. There were voices in that wind, and they continually beckoned to her to come to them, to move deeper into the trees. She didn't want to go to them, so she ran away from the wind, from the voices. Despite her attempts, their suggestions only grew louder and heavier as the night grew darker. Why had she listened to them before? Why, why, *why*?

She felt lost, exposed, vulnerable. She badly wanted to hear her father's voice, for him to soothe her, to convince her that everything would be okay because it was always okay. Dad always protected them from the monsters. Her little brother tugged on her arms, his whimpers cutting through the silence of the woods. Up ahead, there was only darkness and the movement of shadows, trees the lumbering beasts casting them. To her sides was the same, endless nothingness, shades of dark green and gray.

Her brother let go of her arm, and she turned. He was running, not back the way they'd come, but instead making a beeline through the trees and off the pathway they'd made. She yelled at the little boy, shocked at his sudden departure, his sudden courage, his sudden insanity. The boy did not stop. She stood there, too stunned to move, as his outline disappeared into the trees. She dropped to her knees and put her face in her arms. She didn't know what to do without her father.

Eventually, the wind called to her again, telling her to come, telling her that if she followed, she'd find her brother. Feeling hopeless, feeling without options, she listened. She walked as the wind commanded. She stepped over dead tree stumps, dodging branches that she saw too late. She walked carefully now, no longer feeling rushed for escape. She no longer called out to her father, because she'd accepted that he was not coming.

Minutes passed before she entered the clearing. It wasn't an exit from the trees, but a brief solace at their center. The grass was tall here, nearly to her waist, and she had to wade through it to pass, the bottom of her pant legs catching on weeds as she stepped. The wind was blowing at her back now, thrusting her forward and onward, and the blades of grass bent in the same direction to reinforce the wind's message. Soon she approached a man-made structure at the end of the clearing. It was built of concrete, a large rectangular box. Its lid was pulled off to the side, leaned against it. She approached and looked inside, but saw only darkness.

There was a creaking above her as the wind blew. She expected it to be the trees, but subconsciously knew it wasn't. It was a tight creaking sound, not a hollow snap. It was the sound of something that had weight, swinging like a pendulum. Tears streamed down her face as she gained the courage to look. As she did, slowly arching her face upward, she first saw her brother's dirty brown hair, then his vacant green eyes. She yelled out to him as he dangled there just out of reach, but his expression did not change. She saw the reason for his silence. His rib cage had been broken open, spilling his insides into the box below. Her father had butchered many deer from within their garage at home, and this was what her brother was now, as he swung upside down on a rope above her.

She started to scream as his body twisted and rocked in the breeze, and she had long since forgotten about her own safety. She didn't see it when it grabbed her, but she felt everything.

Back at camp, her father was long gone, only their empty tent remaining. He was driving, already several miles away. The wind had told him he didn't have any children, and he believed it. Why would it lie to him about something like that? He needed to get back home to his wife. So he drove all night until, abruptly, the wind stopped talking.

Oh God, he thought, understanding that he'd left his children to the wind and trees.

On the gravel, in his confusion, he lost control of the vehicle and drove into the ditch going eighty. He was flung through the windshield, having left without buckling, and landed in a corn field thirty to forty yards away. It would take someone a day to see the vehicle in the ditch of that rarely used side road, and another day more for the body to be found.

2

Arthur looked in the rearview mirror at Jay, buckled into his booster and playing on his tablet, and thought about how much he loved the boy. Jay smiled as he tapped away at the touchscreen, his chubby, young features illuminated by the screen, features that were beginning to lengthen and tighten as he got older. He wasn't a toddler anymore, was becoming a young boy, and for Arthur, that was both exciting and scary. Little Jay knew his numbers, letters, and was getting better at reading, but he was also beginning to learn how to be a person, too. Arthur desperately hoped he was capable of teaching Jay everything he needed to know about how to be a good person.

It was late in the day and Arthur was driving them to a lake a few hours from home for a weekend of fishing and camping. They were both excited. Arthur felt he was lucky to have a son that loved being outdoors as much as his father did, a son who begged him to go out every weekend and sometimes more. Counting down the days to their next excursion had become an activity between them, and most weekends they'd fish for a few hours in the river near the house or at a lake close by. Those were day trips, though, where they were only out for a few hours and were home in time to clean their catch before dark. This trip would be different. In the back of their truck was a four person tent, a cooler of ice, food, and drinks, a couple sleeping bags, and various other knick knacks that would get them through the next three days "in nature," as Jay called it.

Arthur had found an obscure lake a decent distance away from any towns because he wanted to give himself and Jay the feeling of true isolation, of being alone in wilderness, without taking his son somewhere too dangerous. The lake's website indicated there were open camp sites, free to the public. Arthur had tried calling the number on the website in an attempt to reserve a site, but found the phone line disconnected. To him, this was promising, and he hoped it meant there wouldn't be many people there.

This trip was to be a trial run for Jay, his first big trip. Arthur, on the other hand, was plenty experienced. At least once a year Arthur and a few friends would go canoe camping with nothing more than a backpack each, including their dehydrated food and water filters. In some of the places they went, full of trees and mountains, cell service didn't work, and it brought both a sense of terror and peace. There were few people around and few modern luxuries. When the fear of being alone finally fell away, there was serenity. He'd fish, throw up a hammock, banter with his friends, play cards, and enjoy being alive at an intimately private, personal level. This feeling would last for the duration of the trip, then they would head home. Life would resume.

Arthur wanted to have those same trips with Jay and was eager to get started. He'd been patient so far, letting the kid season, get a little older, a little more mature. Jay had begun showing interest in camping. He had found videos online showing another father and his boys that liked to go hiking and fishing out "in nature." Jay wanted Arthur to take him camping, and Arthur eagerly obliged. The next three days were going to be an opportunity to see if Jay, who was only seven but seemed ahead of his time, was ready. This trip wasn't quite at the backpacking level, but it was a start. Soon it would be only the two of them underneath the stars at night, casting lines in the day. He felt teary-eyed at the thought.

It was difficult for him to explain the impact of becoming a father. When he looked at his son, who was becoming more and more like him every day, yet was still his own little person, he couldn't imagine going back to a life without him. It seemed so lonely. He'd had conversations with Kris, his wife, telling her that even when he felt overwhelmed and like a total failure (he had a decent job, but had a childhood friend who owned a half-million dollar home in Washington D.C.) he'd look at Jay and feel nothing but pride. Even at his worst, Arthur had his little man, this little dude that looked up to him like he was the best person in the world, a little person that wanted nothing more than to spend one whole day with dad.

Arthur wished he could do this with his son more often, and planned to make the most of the trip. At the end of it, he would have to go back to the grind, back to spending half of each day working at a job that had little value to him, a job that was solely a means to a paycheck. Working felt wasteful of his time, something he did because he had to provide. Yet, that was the irony. In order to provide for what mattered (Jay) he had to do what didn't matter (get paid).

It reminded him of his own father. He didn't spend a lot of time with his dad, not like he was able to with Jay. His father had been busy, going to work before Arthur woke up and returning home as Arthur was going to bed. Arthur had been raised primarily by his mother, but not because that's what his father wanted. His father was present in Arthur's life as often as he could make time, teaching him lessons and showing him as many things as he could, things that were still valuable to him today. In order to provide for what mattered (Arthur), his father had to do what didn't matter (get paid). In this way, Arthur was a little more successful than he gave himself credit. He didn't have a big house or an important job, but his simple nine-to-five desk job paid well enough that he could do things like camp on the weekends with his son. His father never had that opportunity, had to work hard right up until the unexpected stroke that took his life.

Arthur often felt as though he'd never compare to his father, could never be as good of a dad as he had been. Even though his father was always at work, in the time they did have together, he'd learned about what it meant to be a person. He wasn't sure how he would do the same for Jay. Ever since his dad had passed, he'd struggled with it internally. He'd considered talking to a therapist about those feelings, just to get another perspective, but never did. At some level he didn't feel like talking to anyone about it, just wanted to try his best and hoped everything worked out in the end, that he didn't fuck it all up with some inept decision.

He thought of life as an elaborate game of Jenga. Each generation of children built off of their parent's accomplishments, if there were any to build from. Children grew up at home, then left, and had the choice of either building up or starting over. Some children dutifully built up from the foundation created by their parents, and the others either laughed as it all crumbled down or looked on confused, wondering why the world was so hard. Arthur was left a decently sized tower, a strong foundation. He desperately wanted to make his father proud by keeping the family tower going. He didn't want to be the one in his ancestry that took out the wrong block and caused everyone's efforts to come crashing down.

It could have been harder, though. Through Kris, his wife, he'd learned what it was like for the people on the other side, children forced to start over, the Jenga pieces a pile in front of them. She'd never known her parents, had grown up in foster care, and didn't have someone guiding her through each of her difficult decisions. But she was smart. She was careful. She made decisions with precision. She grabbed one piece at a time and placed it with purpose. She graduated college, started a job as a teacher, bought a home with Arthur, and now they had Jay and a newborn little girl. Their mission was the same, to ensure their children would start with as sturdy a tower as they could hand them.

He grabbed a bag of seeds next to him from the center console, shook out a handful, and popped them into his mouth. He'd been eating them since they'd left and the salt was turning his cheek raw. His jaw hurt as he chewed, his gut heavy. They'd been on the road for a couple hours now with less than another to go. The sky was a light orange as the sun was finishing its descent. He'd hoped to leave sooner, but with work, he sometimes didn't get that choice.

"Almost there, buddy," he said.

Jay looked up in the mirror and smiled, then went back to his tablet.

"You excited?"

"Well, yes, of course. Are we going to fish when we get there?"

"Probably not tonight. We'll have to get the tent set up first."

"Will we have to set it up in the dark?"

"No, I don't think so, but it will be close."

"Do you know where we're going to set up the tent?"

He had a vague idea of where they'd set up, based on the Google satellite maps. He thought he could make out the campsites from the imaging, but wasn't sure. Like the phone number, everything had seemed out of date. But it wasn't a big deal. He could set up in any clearing as long as the truck could reach it. He kind of hoped the area they found was unexplored. He liked trying new places, new lakes, getting to know what a new area had to offer. Especially small lakes in the middle of nowhere. Fishing the same lakes over and over got boring, and Arthur liked the unknown. He hoped that the lake being small and hidden would mean less people. Whenever Arthur camped in a common location, he regretted it. He hated being forced to set up a few feet from other people, could hear them at night and see them during the day. It didn't ruin the experience, but it did steal a bit from what made camping fun. For Arthur, at least.

"Dad?" Jay asked.

"Yes?"

"You didn't answer."

"What was the question?" Arthur asked. He had a habit of getting lost in his thoughts.

"Do you know where we're going to set up the tent?"

"Oh, I have a spot picked out. Don't worry bud."

"I don't really want to set up in the dark. That sounds scary."

"Don't worry. Maybe we'll make a fire and put up the tent. It'll go up quick."

"And then we'll fish in the morning?"

"You bet."

In his peripheral, he saw a red light appear in the corner of his phone, leaning against the center console running GPS. 15% battery. He'd forgotten to plug it in. He found his charger by feeling around for the cord, then plugged it into the cigarette lighter. This reminded him of riding in his father's truck (everything seemed to remind him of his father these days). While Arthur used the cigarette port as a charger, his father had used it to light his cigarettes, probably the last generation to use it for that purpose. Thinking about it, he could taste the smoke of that first burn vividly in his mind. He'd never smoked, of course. Just another of his father's lessons, just another example of the next generation choosing to build off of the experiences of the last. But man, he'd light one up then if it would help him feel close to his father again.

3

The GPS led him to the lake's only dock and he pulled over. The sky was dark orange, turning purple. An app on his phone that told him the exact time for sun up and sun down indicated he had half an hour of light left. Looking at the lake, he decided to risk it.

"Want to check out the water, bud?"

"Yeah!" Jay said, frantically unbuckling his seat belt.

Arthur opened his truck door and stepped out, his boots grinding as he stood on the gravel. Jay's door slammed and the boy was running to the lake. Arthur followed close behind. There were hollow *pop pop pop* sounds as Jay ran across the plastic dock, then silence as he stood on the edge. Arthur caught up to him and looked around. It was definitely a small lake. He could see all sides of it, apart from an area off to the left that curled around a bend. There were trees surrounding the lake, which felt ominous for no reason at all. Back home in North Dakota, where everything was flat, lakes were often bordered by farmland. The deeper he went into Minnesota, where they were now, that was no longer the case. It usually unsettled him and he wasn't sure why, as if getting away from home was both exciting and worrying. Being surrounded by the trees gave him a feeling of claustrophobia that came and passed, as if he was trapped on the lake and couldn't see beyond it.

"Yup, sunnies!" Jay yelled.

Arthur looked down and stared into the water. It took him a moment, but in time he could see the flutter of shadows underneath the surface as well, even in the darkening afternoon. They were thin, long, black footballs under the water. They looked fairly large, but the surface of the water was always misleading. Jay impressed him. Arthur hadn't been able to identify fish like that at his age. Jay was a bright kid. Jay would certainly make the tower taller when it was his turn to take over.

"Yeah, I see them, too," Arthur said.

"Can we fish now?"

"Not yet, it'll be dark soon. We can come back here in the morning."

"But dad, you said we would fish."

Childish impatience. As Arthur had gotten older, he realized, as most people do, how spread out time was and how much time he actually had. At some point, he stopped saying "let's do it today!" and started saying "tomorrow is fine." He knew Jay would go through it, too, would lose the edge of his childish excitement. But it was all a cycle. After Arthur's father had died, that feeling again changed, as if the sensation of time had altered from permanence to facade. He started realizing that "tomorrow is fine" would have to again become "let's do it today," because time wasn't as eternal as it sometimes felt. *Man, I miss you, dad*, he thought.

"Don't worry. We have all day tomorrow. Do you want to be stuck in the dark?" Arthur asked.

"Why, are there monsters at night?"

"No, but it's still nice to have a tent."

"Are there animals?"

"Well yes, but they won't…"

"Then I don't want to be outside at night," Jay said, a hint of fear in his voice. Arthur would have to break that fear. The boy would be more relaxed by the time they left, he hoped, would have an understanding of how these things worked, that he was safe if he followed the rules and was smart. If Arthur did his job right, at least.

"Don't worry," Arthur said, "Get in the truck. Let's find our campsite and get set up."

They drove down a dirt trail that was overgrown with weeds. Arthur had to steer sharply to avoid a few nasty holes. The makeshift roads likely didn't get much (if any) traffic. Lakes were a dime a dozen in Minnesota. Eventually the trees cleared, exposing a few open camping spots. There was a tent on the far side of the clearing, and Arthur felt disappointed. They'd see people this weekend. The tent was dark and there was no vehicle by it, so maybe it was left behind. He stopped the truck near the campsite furthest from the tent. He unbuckled and opened his door to get out.

"Can I come?" Jay asked.

"Not yet, bud. Let me get us ready. It's already pretty dark. Play on your tablet. Is it still plugged in?"

"Yeah."

"Okay, leave it plugged in so it's charged for the weekend."

He moved to shut the door.

"Dad?" Jay asked just before he slammed the door.

Arthur popped his head back in. "Yeah?"

"I want to know how to set up the tent."

"I'll show you how to take it down when we leave. If you know how to take it down, you'll know how to set it up, too. We'll have more light when we leave. Right now, it's just too dark for you. Stay put for now, okay?"

"You got it, dad."

At the back of the truck, Arthur dropped the tailgate with a thud. It was packed full. He was surprised by how quickly the truck filled with gear. Even more surprising was that he could, somehow, get everything he needed into a single 60 liter backpack when going canoe camping, but still felt like he needed all of this stuff for a few days tent camping with his son. He pushed aside fishing gear, coolers, chairs and cooking supplies and pulled out the tent bag. He found a flat spot for the tent and dropped the bag. The ground wasn't too rough, but wouldn't feel great to sleep on, either. The tent was up as the sun fully disappeared. He took out the sleeping bags, threw them into the tent, and grabbed a flashlight. He opened Jay's door. Jay, who was focused on his game, jumped in surprise. Arthur laughed.

"Don't laugh! You scared me," Jay said.

"Aright, bud, bring your tablet and let's get some shut eye."

The boy yawned and drug himself out of the truck. Arthur slammed the door, then walked around to take out the keys. He locked the vehicle out of habit, then got into the tent behind Jay. A few mosquitoes had already gotten inside, were bobbing stupidly at the top of the tent. He rolled out both sleeping bags. Jay quickly crawled inside his, turned off his tablet, and promptly went to sleep. The boy was an early sleeper and an early riser. Arthur was not. As he pulled himself inside his bag and laid down, the ground hurt his back, a painful reminder that he was aging. When exactly did that start? His back hadn't hurt like that last year. He shifted in the bag until he found a position that was bearable. He decided to text his wife, scolding himself for not calling sooner.

Hey, I'm sorry. We just got here. Tent is set up. Jay is asleep already.

No response came, and the indicator didn't show read. She was likely asleep. Back home, Arthur was always the last one asleep, too.

It was beautifully quiet outside, the only sounds being crickets and bugs chirping. There were no cars, no police sirens, no societal static, no noise from the other tent. Even when things were quiet in town, he swore he could still hear the radiation of thousands of people in one area. It was the sound of stress and chaos. Sitting there, alone with his son "in nature," was the good life. This was how living was meant to be. At least until the food ran out and they had to go home.

With peace in his mind, he fell asleep.

4

"Dad! It's light out. Can we go fishing?"

Arthur opened his eyes, seeing Jay staring down at him. It was chilly in the tent, and Arthur wrapped the sleeping bag tighter around his body, dipping his chin inside closer to the warmth of his cocoon. "Jesus, what time is it?"

Jay was quiet, focused on his tablet, then started reading off the numbers. "7...4...5...."

Arthur reached around the inside of his bag until he found his phone. 7:45. A little late for Jay to be up, actually. No message back yet from Kris, who'd likely sleep in with the baby for as long as she could with Jay out of the house.

"Why do you wake up so early?" Arthur asked.

"I just wake up, I can't help it. Let's go fishing."

"Jesus, give me a moment."

His back was killing him. He hated getting older. He wanted to be in his twenties again, though thirty-four wasn't that old and shouldn't feel this rough. Was he that out of shape, or did stuff really start breaking down that early? He didn't remember his father showing weakness, even in his fifties. He wondered if Jay noticed the pain his dad was in, or if he saw his father as invincible, too. He shifted his body until the pain eased. His bladder burned.

"Dad. I'm bored."

"Where's your tablet?"

"There's no internet."

"Do all your games require the internet?" He remembered the handheld games he had when he was little, which were never connected to the internet. He almost brought that up to Jay, but the thought of being *that* kind of generational stereotype, a dad reflecting on the good ole days, stopped him. There was nothing wrong with the advance of time, but complaining about it certainly came easy once time started moving on.

"The fun ones need internet, and I can't download new ones. Unless you want to play chess. I have an app to play chess, but the game doesn't have a computer to play against."

"I hate that game. What kind of kid your age likes chess." He rubbed sleep from his eyes. They were sticky, and he had to wipe the corners of his eyes a few times to get all the gunk out.

"Grandma plays with me. She says it'll make me smart."

Arthur laughed, "I suppose she's right. I'm not very good at it. Grandpa always beat me." He sat up, the sleeping bag falling from his chest. A wave of icy air hit his skin. He didn't have enough hair on his chest yet to keep him warm, it seemed. Old enough for aches, but not enough for a warm, hairy body.

"I'll be smart like grandpa, then," Jay said.

"You already are, buddy."

"Okay, let's go." Jay said. He unzipped the tent.

"God damn, give me a moment," Arthur said, but it was too late. The boy was gone. "Grab the duffel bag from the back of the truck!" He yelled out after Jay.

5

Once they were both dressed in fresh clothes, they walked to the edge of the water nearest camp, Jay carrying his fishing rod, Arthur carrying his and the tackle bag. The shoreline was a short hike from their campsite, and it wasn't a bad fishing spot. There were few weeds, and large rocks to sit on.

"We're pretty lucky, Jay. This looks like a good spot already."

"If it's not, can we go to the dock?"

"Sure."

They found the largest and flattest rock and sat down together. Arthur set up his son's line. A bare hook, a worm, and a weight. This is how he always had his son start, since it was the perfect set up for all sorts of small fish in the shallows. If Jay wanted to start casting, he'd give him a jig and a worm, but usually the boy was content with a bare hook. Within seconds the sunnies were hitting the boy's line, and he brought one up.

"I'm a better fisherman than you, dad," Jay said as he took the hook out of the fish's mouth, "I caught the first fish."

"Yeah you are," Arthur said, "but that one's a little small. We'll throw him back."

"No, I don't want to, I want to keep him," Jay begged.

The boy would keep every fish if he could. He hadn't learned yet that the effort to keep small fish and clean them was not worth it, nor was it rewarding. They weren't desperate for food. They didn't need the fish. Fishing was about the reward of the catch, to catch bigger and bigger fish and to refine a skill. His father had taught him that, though not through fishing. His father taught him that through actions like helping people, when he could. The reward was the act, how it made you feel, not the prize or any material value in return. Best send the small fish back to get bigger. They fished in silence for some time, eventually catching fish big enough to keep for their meal that night.

"Dad, did you hear those sounds last night?" Jay asked in between a cast. He'd been staring into the water quietly for a while, but that wasn't uncommon. The kid was constantly lost in thought, when he wasn't asking endless questions. The apple doesn't fall far from the tree, as they say.

"No, I was asleep all night. Did you wake up? What sounds? Were you dreaming?"

"I don't think so. It woke me up, so I listened to it. I thought it was you snoring at first, but you weren't snoring."

"Did it sound like an animal? Maybe a squirrel or something?"

"No, it didn't sound like that. It sounded like... a low hum at first, then it was talking almost. But I couldn't understand it."

"Maybe the wind, a breeze?" The sound of wind against the tent must be weird to him, Arthur thought, but that didn't seem right. He'd been camping before. Maybe it was windier last night than usual. Arthur slept hard, and would have slept through any rattling of the tent. "There is that tent. Maybe those people were up late."

"I don't think it was wind. It started for a while, then stopped. I guess it could have been those people. I almost went outside to see what it was, but got scared of the dark."

Arthur's heart rate spiked. The thought of Jay alone in the woods while he slept unaware back inside the tent terrified him. The total helplessness of it, of Jay getting lost out there, Arthur not finding out until he awoke the next morning.

"Jay, don't ever leave the tent without me. Do you understand?"

"Why? Monsters?"

He had to keep his tone calm, but inside he was rattled. Jay was the most important person in Arthur's life now, and the thought of something happening to the boy was unthinkable. He thought about scaring the boy a bit, bringing up animals like bears or foxes that could hurt him, but decided that would take it too far. He didn't want the boy terrified. He needed him to be smart and alert is all. He needed him to understand the danger, but not fear it. He chose his words carefully.

"I don't want you to get hurt or lost in the trees. You could wander too far and I'd never be able to find you," Arthur said.

"I wouldn't do that, dad. I'd stay by the tent."

"Jay, promise me. Promise me that you won't leave the tent without me."

"Okay, I promise."

"Seriously, Jay. If you feel the urge to leave, you need to wake me up."

"I will dad. I promise."

Arthur wasn't satisfied by the answer, but knew he'd gotten all he could without tainting the boy's joy of camping. He decided that he'd move the sleeping bags around. That would force Jay to crawl over him to get outside. That made him feel better, the risk minimized.

6

They got back to camp a little after two, starving and ready to eat. Jay would have stayed down by the shore for several more hours, but Arthur pulled him away. The kid was stubborn and insistent, all good traits for later in life. But in the moment, Arthur was hungry, which was more important.

"We're here all weekend, Jay. We'll try other spots. Probably after lunch."

"But I was getting bites, and we caught fish at that spot."

"Yes, but it's more about getting a feel for the lake, finding more good spots."

"So you can get even bigger fish?"

"Yes. If you fish in one spot every time, how do you know what else is out there?"

"That's true, dad. Maybe we can try down by the dock from last night."

"Sure, we can try there."

Moments like this made Arthur feel like a good father, made him feel like he maybe, possibly, was growing that tower taller. He hoped he was imparting good wisdom to Jay, and not something that would hold him back later in life. Not in that particular moment, but in general. He knew there were lessons he wasn't aware of himself passing.

They'd kept a few good sized perch between 9 and 11 inches. Enough for a meal. Jay had continued catching sunnies, but Arthur, after continued argument, convinced him to throw them all back. Some were decently sized for sunnies, but cleaning sunnies was not something Arthur felt like doing. They were more rib cage than meat. He'd hoped for some walleye or pike, bigger fish with more meat, but it wasn't in the cards. He was confident their luck would change when they ventured out. He cleaned the fish, then fried the fillets with butter and salt over the fire. He took out a couple bags of chips and bottles of water.

After their meal, they burned the fish remains, but Arthur was sure to explain that they couldn't do this everywhere they camped. There wasn't a concern for bears where they were at, from what he'd read online, but if they ever camped where there were bears, it was important to bury waste far away. It wasn't worth the risk of attracting predators. They relaxed by the fire, enjoying the peace and quiet. The sun made them hot, then the breeze cooled them down in a back and forth exchange. That was something Arthur often took for granted, the consistent temperature of an indoor home. Outside, it seemed he was always fluctuating between too hot or too cold, with fleeting moments of feeling perfect. He wondered if that was normal, or an indicator of a blood pressure problem.

"Hey, dad."

"What's up?"

"That tent from yesterday is gone."

He looked across to the other campsite and noticed the same. He hadn't realized it before. Having camped many times before, he'd gotten into the habit of ignoring other campers as if they were background noise.

"Yeah, you're right."

"I never heard them leave."

"Me either. They must have left when we were fishing."

"Yeah true. Too bad we didn't get to say goodbye," Jay said.

"Yes, too bad," Arthur said. A shame. Truly a shame.

7

Before bed, they fished briefly at the dock. They caught nothing worth keeping, all small sunnies, and Jay was deeply disappointed. Arthur, who didn't feel like cleaning more fish, was okay with it.

8

That night, Arthur moved around the sleeping bags to block the exit, and Jay didn't question him.

"If you hear stuff outside, what should you do?" Arthur asked, testing the boy.

"Wake you up."

"Do you ever go outside alone?"

"No, dad."

"Alright, good. Want to talk to mom for a bit before bed?"

"Yes!"

They called, and gave her an update on the day. Jay talked about his fish, and said he was liking his time away with dad. Mom missed them both, and was getting bored at home without them. Arthur said it was only a couple more nights, she shouldn't worry about them, and to make sure the doors were locked. After the call was over, Jay was soon snoring, and Arthur let himself fall asleep, too.

9

In the middle of the night, Jay woke him up. "Dad, the noises."

"What noises?"

"They've been going on for a while now, but they're much louder now, just outside the tent."

Arthur paused, listening. He heard nothing, and his eyelids felt heavy. "There's nothing out there, bud. Go to sleep."

"Dad," Jay whispered, "Just wait."

He did, willing his eyelids to halt their retreat. Still, there was nothing. Then he heard it. A rustling of empty chip bags. They'd left them out, and something was helping itself to the leftovers. Arthur held his body as still as he could, not wanting to make any sounds that might attract whatever was out there. He wasn't sure what it was. Surely it wasn't a bear. Even so, doubt nagged at the back of his mind, the worry that a bear could be right outside the tent and that his son was in danger. He'd never seen a bear while camping, but figured their breathing was loud and grunt-like. He pulled his wood chopping ax out from underneath his pillow (he always took it to the tent with him while sleeping) and got on his knees.

"Dad? What are you doing?"

He needed to scare away whatever was out there, but didn't want his son to get hurt, either. Could it try to get into the tent? Arthur felt trapped between two difficult necessities, to get out and scare away the animal but also to keep his son safe. Either way, he had to do something. He unzipped the top part of the zipper on the door and looked out, hoping to see whatever it was. If he was wrong and it was a bear, hopefully he'd get a quick glance at the size of the thing. He saw only blackness.

"Dad?" Jay asked again.

"Everything's okay," he whispered back into the tent, "There's just a small animal out there eating our food." Arthur was guessing, but figured it was most likely true. "I've gotta go scare it away, okay?"

"Okay," Jay said with a waver in his voice.

"Don't worry, this happens all the time. I'm going to go out there, scare it, clean up the garbage, and come back in, okay?"

"Okay."

"I need you to stay in here and leave the zipper up. I'll be right back."

Jay nodded, tears in his eyes. Arthur paused and watched the boy for a bit. This might scar him, he worried. Either way, this was a reality when camping, and this was why they were practicing. Jay had to be ready for this if they were to go on longer, more dangerous trips.

"Hey, it's okay buddy. Don't worry. I'd never let anything happen to you."

"I know."

He didn't like knowing the boy was scared. "Jay," he said, "Did you know that if you're really still, really quiet, most animals can't see or hear you?" It wasn't true, but it was kind of true. He could fix it later, but in the moment he wanted to reassure the boy. "So you being in here is the safest place, right? Just stay really still, and really quiet, and nothing can hurt you."

Jay smiled. A weak smile, but it was something. "Okay, dad."

"Okay, I'll be right back. Stay here and hang tight."

Arthur lowered the zipper to the ground and stepped into the cool night, immediately missing the warmth of his sleeping bag. He wondered how goofy he looked, a father gaining weight, standing outside in his underwear. He stepped around the outside of the tent cautiously, looking for anything that was out there, for the shine of an animal's eyes in the moonlight. He saw nothing at either the table, the fire (now burnt embers), or by the truck. Whatever the thing was, it had scampered away.

He walked over to where the food had been and saw much of it torn into. Bags of chips were spread out across the ground and ripped open. Bread bags had bite marks with pieces torn out. The animal had been frenzied and hungry. He scooped up what was still good and threw it back into a storage bin. The rest he put into a garbage bag, then tied it and threw it into the back of the truck. He put the storage bin with the food back as well, as he should have done before bed. It had been a stupid mistake, one out of carelessness. There may not be bears in the area, but he still should have been smarter. Now his son was scared.

He stood there for a moment, staring into the back of the truck, thinking about Jay, and grabbed something small out from one of the other bins. He closed the truck bed. When he returned to the tent, Jay was lying in his sleeping bag.

"Hey, you okay buddy?" Arthur asked.

"Yeah, I'm okay." The boy still sounded nervous, but less nervous than before.

"It was just a raccoon. We'll have to make sure we clean up better before bed."

"Okay. Thank you dad."

"I got something for you." He took out the small pocket knife he'd taken from the bin in the back of the truck. He showed him how to open and close it, then handed it to him. "This is really dangerous. You know when you play with the campfire, how careful you have to be so you don't burn yourself?"

"Yeah."

"It's the same with this. You can hurt yourself or someone else really bad with it. But it can also make you safe. Now, if an animal gets close to you, you have something to use just in case. But only use it if you're in danger. Do you understand?"

"Yes, dad. Thank you." His smile was wide. Arthur hoped he hadn't made a mistake, but trusted his gut.

"When we get home, I'll have to take that away, though. It's only for camping."

"I understand, dad."

He nodded his head, then got back into his sleeping bag and quickly warmed back up. The things were marvelous in their ability to retain heat.

"Dad?"

"Yeah?"

"Can raccoons whisper?"

"I'm actually not sure what sounds they make. I think it's more like a scratching sound. Like the sounds rats or mice make." He made a mental note to look it up in the morning.

"So those other sounds I've been hearing, I don't think it was the raccoon."

"What do you mean?"

"I don't know. Before I heard the raccoon out there, there was talking. Yesterday it was really quiet, but today it sounded more and more like a person whispering to me through the tent. It stopped when the raccoon came."

Arthur didn't know how to respond to this. He was positive it was nothing more than the wind. There was nothing else it could be. The people from the other tent had left. Despite this, Arthur still felt uneasy.

"Let's talk about it in the morning, bud, sound good?"

"Sure, dad."

10

Arthur woke to the sound of his son playing on his tablet. The air tasted wet and birds chirped outside. He took a moment to soak in the serenity before sitting up. It hurt his back to do so, and he had to pause halfway up to let everything catch up. He didn't believe in the science of chiropractic care, but he did believe in the placebo effect, and felt he should make an appointment when they got back home.

"Hey bud, how'd you sleep?"

"Okay. I need to charge my tablet."

Noted, he thought. His phone probably needed a charge as well. He'd left it on battery-saver since they'd arrived, but that usually only gave it another day and a half before needing a charge. "We'll charge them in the car for a bit today."

"Okay." The boy didn't look up from the tablet. He must have found games he could play without the internet.

"Alright, let's throw together a breakfast and figure out what to do with the day."

"Find a new fishing spot?" Jay asked.

"You bet."

He fried up eggs on the portable griddle and smoked sausage links over the fire. He loved that smell, and the task of cooking even more. He needed this. He hoped his son would continue to want to do it, too. Arthur started the truck and plugged in the devices to charge while the food cooked. They ate and checked the fishing bags, organizing their laziness from the day before (lures never made it in the right spot when packing up for the day). They cleaned camp, catching everything Arthur had missed in his scramble the night before. Then he grabbed his phone and turned off the truck, and they headed for the trees.

He'd decided they would walk along the shore for a bit. They could drive around the lake, but Arthur thought walking would be a better experience for Jay. So far, Jay had done surprisingly well, and hadn't complained. The trees near camp were fairly spread out, but were tightly tangled in some areas. They had to get creative when walking through some dense spots, with Arthur holding branches back for Jay. In a few instances, Arthur was worried his fishing rod would snap when it got caught on twigs and bent, but so far they'd gotten lucky. Usually around lakes that were commonly fished, there were paths along the shore from fishermen foot traffic, but this was not one of those lakes. They had to make their own painful paths. Come to think of it, he hadn't seen anyone else fishing since they'd gotten there. No people, no boats. He liked it, but to see no one at all out on a weekend was a little bizarre. They reached a small clearing.

"Let's cut in and see what the shore looks like here," Arthur said.

"Okay."

When they reached the water, they found a weedy, shallow mess. He took Jay's hand and walked him down the hill to the muddy shoreline. They wouldn't be able to cast beyond the weeds and would have to fish top water. It might be possible to snag some pike, maybe even a nice bass, but when he thought about it, he didn't feel like dealing with Jay's snags. He'd be frequently re-setting the boy's line.

"I don't like this spot, what do you think?"

"Yuck, too many weeds. It stinks."

"Yup. Let's keep walking around here. It looks better a little ways up."

They climbed back up the shore and kept walking, deeper into the woods. In the monotony of the walk, Arthur's thoughts wandered back to his conversation with his son the previous night, and his questions about the talking voices. "Jay, last night, you said you'd heard the whispering sounds. What do you think it was?" He asked.

"Well, it had to be the wind. That's what you said it was."

"I know, I just want to know what you think it was, before we decided it was the wind."

"Well, it didn't sound like wind. Wind is like... *whoosh*," he said, mimicking the sound and emphasizing with his hands. "This sounded like a person talking so quiet you can't hear. Like Great Grandpa John. But Grandpa John talks like that because he's old and tired, right? I don't think this person was old and tired."

Standing there in the silence of the woods, alone with his son, Arthur regretted asking. "What do you think the voice was saying?"

"It was hard to hear. At first, it didn't sound like words, but eventually I think I heard it asking me to find it."

"You remember what I said about that, right?"

"Yes, I know that dad, you told me yesterday. Stay in the tent. Wake you up. Plus, there's raccoons out there and I can't deal with that."

Arthur laughed. "Good, I don't want you wandering around without me. I still don't think it was anything, I was just curious what it was you thought you heard is all. If you hear the voice again, tell me, and tell me what it says."

"Okay."

11

They'd come to a tough patch to cross, with dead fallen trees and sharp branches. It took Arthur some time to find a spot he deemed safe enough for Jay to cross. Once they did, they found a clearing on the other side that seemed to lead to the lake. As Arthur approached what should have been the shore, though, he was surprised. It wasn't a shore, but instead a sharp drop off into the lake maybe twenty feet below. It would be difficult to get down that steep edge. If he were alone, maybe, but not with Jay. What didn't make sense was that it hadn't felt like they were climbing. He figured he would have felt burning in his calves. Arthur looked ahead along the edge of the lake to see if the drop off continued, or if they should head back to camp. From what he could see, they would walk back down the hill soon, and would have more level ground for fishing. He decided to continue.

"Looks like we have to keep walking, bud. You getting tired yet?"

"Well, a little. Are we almost there?"

"Yes, we're getting there. Just a little longer."

They stepped back into the trees, a safe distance from the drop off. They couldn't see the shore with how thick the trees were in this area. They seemed to be getting thicker, and Arthur began questioning the act of continuing in this direction. He checked his phone. He was shocked to find that it was already two. The day wasn't progressing as he'd hoped, and he felt bummed to be wasting their second day like this. He was dropping the ball and was disappointed in himself. Nothing he could do about it now, though. They'd likely have to skip lunch that day in favor of a bigger and earlier dinner. He wouldn't tell Jay that. He had snacks in his bag for when the boy got hungry.

Soon, they were in another clearing, this time with weeds nearly knee high. Arthur was beginning to feel frustrated. The lake made no sense. He felt turned around. He was looking toward the shoreline, trying to find it, but couldn't see anything beyond the trees at the edge of the clearing.

"Dad, what is that thing?" Jay asked, pointing deep into the clearing.

Arthur looked back at his son, then followed his gaze, and saw it off in the distance. It seemed to be a large stone monument. It looked out of place against the trees and greenery. Things made by man usually did. "Oh, I don't know. That's weird. Let's go check it out."

When they reached the monument, he found it to be a simple square box made of concrete. He was reminded of when he and his siblings were together, when they were making plans to put their father into the ground. They were sitting around a large table with the funeral director who was talking but not really saying anything. It was something about options for how they wanted to present their father's corpse, including the kinds of sandwiches they wanted to offer the onlookers at "the viewing", and color schemes for the pamphlet.

At the time, the moment had struck Arthur because of how surreal it had been. Not only had dad just died, but the funeral home wanted to market an event. Their father's big day, his big send off, inviting as many people as possible to come say goodbye and check out how well the embalmer did. Of course, they never did very well. The body always looked like a wax rendition of the person it once housed. Arthur wasn't religious, but he had faith. The soul was gone and a husk was all that was left behind. A candy bar wrapper might hold the faint shape of what had been inside, but you can still usually tell that it's just an empty piece of plastic.

The memory came to him because the concrete box reminded him of purchasing dad's coffin. Not specifically the coffin, but the box the coffin was stored inside. Initially, they'd chosen a coffin that was humble and simple, fitting for dad, but after they selected the coffin they were asked to select a vault. Optional, of course, but highly recommended. Arthur had never seen or heard about a vault before, and learned that it was an important aspect of the burial process. Over time, the coffin, under the stress of the earth and due to moisture and rot, would fracture and collapse inward. If they wanted to protect their father's husk, they needed a large concrete box surrounding the coffin to support it indefinitely. The spirit would forever be gone, wherever spirits go, but the body would be protected for eternity within that concrete box. Without a vault, they were warned, after ten, twenty, thirty years, they'd eventually visit the grave only to find a sink hole leading to the body.

The concrete box in front of Arthur now was similar in appearance to that vault, but twice its size. Arthur stepped around the box and was shocked to find a thirty to forty foot drop to the lake water below. His mind rocked, his brain floating in unsteady water. How had that small hill they'd been on become a mountain? He looked back to find Jay climbing on top of the large concrete box, approaching the edge.

"Jay, stay back."

"Why, what is it dad?" He continued approaching, his shoes clacking on the concrete.

"Don't come any closer. There's a drop off on this side."

The boy stopped, looking at him.

"It's okay, but there's a sharp drop here. If you were to fall, you'd get very badly hurt. Stay on the other side of this thing."

"Okay," Jay said and turned around. He jumped off the box, back safely on the other side.

Arthur walked around to stand by his son and examined the box. There were no markings, no engravings. It was a simple concrete structure, with a concrete lid sitting on top. The lid was smooth and rounded on the edges, but didn't have handles to move it. He remembered dad's having steel handles that were dried into the concrete. He didn't think this was any kind of coffin, because there were no markers and it was too big, but it looked very much like a vault. He couldn't get that comparison out of his mind.

"Dad, it's open a little," Jay said. Arthur's gaze followed his son's. "There's a gap here, like this is a lid and someone tried to open it. Or close it"

It was true. There was a small black space in the corner of the box closest to them, and the top was slightly askew. His hands brushed along the surface, feeling for something, but it was smooth concrete everywhere he touched. A large concrete box easily large enough to house a few adult bodies, randomly placed in the middle of a clearing, atop a mountain that hadn't been there that morning. He found himself wishing he'd spent more time researching the lake. Arthur caught Jay reaching his hand into the hole and stopped him.

"Jay, use your head. There could be something in there. Think before you act." *Think before you act.* Another lesson from dad, now passed to the next generation.

"Sorry dad." His hands dropped to his sides, but Jay was still staring into the hole. "Think we could push the lid off? See what's in there?" Jay eventually asked.

"I don't think that's a good idea, bud."

"Do you think there's a body? Is this a coffin, like grandpa's?"

Interesting, Arthur thought. The boy was making the same connection he was. "I don't think so. It's too big. But if it was, do you think we should disturb it?"

"No, probably not. That wouldn't be very nice."

"Right, exactly."

The child looked bewildered, still curious, but considering what he'd been told. "Well, could we shine a light in the gap?"

Arthur thought about this. He had to admit to himself that he was curious, too, but something still felt wrong. Even so, the lid on the thing would weigh a ton. If there was something in it, then it was trapped. He took out his phone and turned on the flashlight. "Stand back," he said. Jay stood back, excitement in his eyes. Arthur shone the light into the gap. He started at one corner and rotated the phone inch by inch. At first he saw nothing. It was exactly as it seemed, a large, empty concrete box. Eventually, however, his eyes adjusted to the limited sliver of what he could see at a time, and the outline of the contents became more clear. He scanned slowly left. In the corner, he could see dirt on the ground and what looked like vegetation or roots. The vegetation had grown up through the bottom of the box. "What in the world," he whispered to himself, trying to figure out what the box was for.

"What is it dad? Is it a body?"

"No, it looks empty..." He started, but the light flashed across something that had a different texture, something more dull and smooth than the root-covered ground. It was hard to focus with such a small area. He had to fight with his big head and the position of the phone to find the ideal angle of light. Once he found a good resting point, and his eyes adjusted again, he found that he was looking at the dried skin of a face. A very large, bulbous, dead-looking face. He leapt back, startled. There was a corpse inside.

"What is it, dad? Can I see?"

"No, bud. There's... There's nothing in there. Just a box with dirt and roots."

"Oh, then what scared you?"

"Nothing, I had an itch is all," he said, and began to itch his right eye. Jay gave him a disbelieving look. The wind seemed to be picking up. Arthur looked at his phone. It was past four. "Are you hungry?"

"Well yes, a little bit."

"Okay, let's get back to camp and make some food."

"But we were going to fish!" Jay said, ready to throw a fit.

Arthur wasn't in the mood to deal with that. "I know, but we ended up walking for too long. Now we know not to come this way tomorrow, right? Come on, let's go."

Arthur was ready to pack up and leave the lake. There was nothing wrong, but the body and the vault had unsettled him. Why was there an unburied coffin here, of all places? This along with the odd geography of the lake unsettled him. Something didn't feel right.

12

They made their way back through the trees, the wind picking up and howling as they walked. The trees swayed and leaves rustled. Arthur wasn't lost, but he felt lost, and it was taking longer than it should to get back to camp. He hated this lake more with each passing second. He decided they'd leave that night.

"Dad, the wind... It's talking again."

"What?"

"Don't you hear it?"

He stopped walking and stood quietly. He could hear the leaves, the rush of air against his ears, but nothing else. It sounded like wind to him.

"No, it's just wind, Jay."

"Okay," the boy said, and was quiet.

Arthur was certain they were going back the same way they had come that morning, but things looked different, and they should have arrived at the campsite by now. He pulled out his phone and opened his GPS. Thankfully, in the modern age, there were enough satellites that GPS seemed to work just about everywhere, even in the most remote places he'd been, even when he didn't have enough signal to make a call. When the map loaded, he stared at it in confusion, because what he saw didn't make sense. They were on the opposite side of the lake from camp. Since they'd left the clearing, they hadn't been going back the way they'd come at all. Somehow they'd been moving in the *opposite* direction entirely, away from camp, continuing their trek around the lake. How had that happened? How could he possibly have gotten that turned around?

He wondered if he was looking at the map wrong. He moved it around with his fingers, found the spot with the dock, then located the campsite. No, he wasn't wrong. They were indeed on the other side of the lake. How? *How?*

It didn't matter. He had to get them back before dark so they could pack. They could turn around and walk back the way they came, but that didn't seem worth the effort. It would take just as long to go that way, and they'd have to cross paths with the concrete box again, not to mention walk up that mountain while they were tired. He'd rather not be near any of it. However, continuing was also a risk, as he didn't know what he'd find in front of them. He took a deep breath to steady himself. He'd keep his phone open, he decided, and they'd keep walking. The GPS might lose connection occasionally, but he'd generally be able to make sure they stayed on the right path back to camp.

"Okay, bud. Bad news," he said and turned around to face his son.

Jay was gone.

His heart sank and he felt a rock plummet into his gut. He looked around the trees, but couldn't see the boy. He couldn't hear him, either. Only the wind beating against the trees, wind that had somehow gotten unbearably loud.

He'd been in this position before, with Jay missing. It was terrifying losing sight of him, even for a second. Up to this point, however, Jay had always reappeared nearby. Arthur calmed his nerves with steady breaths, forced himself to relax, forced himself to stay quiet and to listen. The boy couldn't have gone far. This surely wouldn't be one of those tragic scenarios where a parent lost their child. He wouldn't be on the news, someone people rumored about under their breath with a *How could he let that happen?* Or a *That would never happen to anyone I know.*

"Jay, where are you bud?" he called.

No answer.

He was frozen in place and didn't know what to do. If he moved too far, and Jay returned, Jay wouldn't have a phone to call someone. He also wouldn't be able to find the way back to camp on his own. Yet, Arthur knew that if he didn't move, if he didn't walk in some direction, his son could continue wandering further and further away. In a couple more hours it would be night, and Jay would be stuck out there.

Fuck, fuck, fuck.

"Jay, answer me bud. Where are you?"

No answer.

He suddenly wished for the comfort of more people being around him, more eyes to look for a lost child. He scanned the ground, looking for tracks, but who was he kidding? He wasn't a tracker. He was a stupid father that liked to pretend he could survive in the wilderness. A stupid father that put his son in danger for no reason other than to have a fun, new experience. Stupid, stupid, *stupid*. His father would have never done something like this. His father always had a plan, could always see around the corner. His father was smart. Arthur was nothing more than a child pretending to be a parent. He missed Jay already and wanted to see him, to hear his voice again.

Call 911. Get someone out here.

He lifted his phone to dial, but as he held the device in his hand, he couldn't remember why he'd pulled it out.

He stared at the screen, the serene background of his lock screen.

He'd come out to this area to find a fishing spot, he knew, and he hadn't found one. He was heading back to the campsite to pack up and leave.

Why did he need his phone again?

The GPS, he remembered. He'd gotten a bit lost, and needed the map to help guide him back to camp. He unlocked the phone, watched the triangle that pointed in the direction he was walking. He began to walk, watching the triangle as it moved toward camp. He felt excited to get home. He missed his wife. He'd enjoyed camping, but was ready to be home and in his own bed.

As he walked, eager to get back, the wind was gradually getting stronger and stronger. He wondered if there'd be a storm soon. He looked up at the clouds. The sky was gray and overcast, but he didn't get the feeling there'd be any rain. He was lucky. It was just a windy day was all. The sun was going down. It would be night soon. He had a long way to walk yet, and realized he'd likely be packing up at night. It wasn't ideal, but it would be fine.

He heard something in the wind and stopped walking. It sounded like a child's voice. As he listened, the voice became more clear.

"Dad," the voice screamed, "Dad! Where are you?"

Dad? He didn't remember seeing a family out here camping.

"Dad! Help!"

The voice sounded familiar, but he couldn't place it.

"Dad, the box," the voice said, "The wind, it lies!"

The box. He remembered the box. The box that his father had lied in. The box the corpse had been in. The box he'd found in the middle of the trees with... *Jay!* Arthur shook his head. What was wrong with him? His head felt foggy and heavy. He'd been walking away from his son. How long had he been walking?

"Jay!" Arthur yelled out, "Jay, where are you?" He paused, listening. There was no response, so he began to run back, back in the direction of the voice. Tree branches scratched at his arm as he ran. In his heart, he knew where he was going, what he was going back to. Jay had returned to the box, or at least in the area of the box. The wind was the voice of the dead thing inside, and it had Jay. He could feel it in his mind still, as it tried to make him forget again. Arthur wouldn't.

"Jay, am I getting closer?" He yelled, but there was no response. "Jay, answer me!"

He desperately hoped he was close to the box, to the clearing. He no longer knew if he was running toward the voice, hadn't heard it in so long, but still he knew where Jay had gone. He ran, pushing himself to run faster. Branches were cutting his arms, but he paid them no mind. He'd have time for pain later.

As the trees thinned, he saw that he'd made it. The clearing stood before him. The concrete box was there at the far end, the night sky a backdrop behind it as it stood atop the hill. He stepped near the box carefully, looking around, not sure what to expect. Soon he saw Jay lying against it on the ground. He couldn't see the boy well, but his hair seemed covered in something dark. Blood? Dirt? His eyes were closed. His hands were tied together by what looked like vines or roots.

He would have run towards Jay, but what he saw stopped him. There was a large creature, much larger than a person, standing in front of the box, between him and Jay. He'd been so focused on Jay that he hadn't seen the creature standing off to the side. Arthur's jaw dropped and the air in his lungs unwillingly escaped. The creature, a giant a few feet taller and much bigger in size than Arthur, was stacking wood, seemingly to make a fire. Its appearance was unlike anything Arthur had seen before, with tight leathery skin and a bony form. It was naked and thin, seemed to be lacking muscle, but Arthur didn't doubt its strength. Its features were long and stretched, lanky almost. It seemed human, but a sick variation of it. A walking giant's corpse. A husk, living without the burden of a soul. Arthur looked at the box again and saw that the lid had slid off and was leaned against it.

"Relax. I won't harm you," the husk said, its voice rough, hoarse, airy.

The sound rattled Arthur, his opportunity for a surprise attack gone.

"Come. Stand closer. We can talk," it said, "I'm surprised. It's rare that you guys come back. Usually you just... leave."

Arthur approached with slow steps, eyes darting between the husk and Jay, who was still unconscious. He got as close as he dared, a triangle forming between the three of them. The husk used stones to spark the dry kindle it had placed into the center of its pile of wood. It blew and the wind howled. Sparks grew from spots of light into small flames.

"Who are you?" Arthur asked

"Not a who. Not a person, not an animal. Just... a *thing* that exists."

"You're just... a thing?" Arthur asked.

"I don't have a name. Naming things is a human behavior. If you need a name you can understand, call us Child Eaters," it said, looking into Arthur's eyes, nothing but a vacant blackness in their center.

Arthur felt as though he might pass out. He was shaking, adrenaline noticeable now that he wasn't running. The husk set down one of the stones he'd used to spark the fire and grabbed another that had a sharper point. It began hitting the dull stone it still held against the sharp one intentionally. Sharpening it? A tool for cutting.

"We can talk while I prepare tools. You're free to leave whenever you like, but your child will stay. If you make a move toward him, I will gut you and hang your body in a tree. I would recommend leaving. I assure you that as you walk away, you'll forget he ever existed. It'll be easier that way. The wind will unburden you of memory."

Jay was still out. Was he already dead? Would he ever wake? A memory of the boy the day before, happily fishing for sunnies, flashed in his mind. *Dad, help me,* Arthur begged in his mind, seeing the parallel to what Jay had also requested moments before, both of them ready for their fathers to save them.

"Usually he'd be gutted by now, but I'm fat and slow from a recent meal, and my tools are dull from the cutting. I was ready to rest when you both stumbled upon me. Thank you for that."

He paused, but Arthur had nothing to say, still feeling stunned and at a loss for words.

"There are more of me, you know," it said, happy to share its tale now that it had an audience, "Everywhere. In places you wouldn't think to look. Some of us like the cold, others the heat. Some in cities, some," it looked up and gestured around, "the trees. There's food for us everywhere. Children are easy prey. We offer simple suggestions, and they come running along, curious as ever. Their fear is limited. They don't yet know horror, don't understand the necessity of caution."

The stone knife was taking shape as it spoke. It wouldn't be long. It was crude, but Arthur could tell that it would enter flesh easily enough. Arthur wanted to take the stone blade and shove it through its neck, but knew he had to be careful. As soon as Arthur appeared to be a threat, the husk would kill him, discard him, and then Jay would be next. Jay's death would be more excruciating, surely. Children roamed unaware while monsters waited everywhere, and Arthur had delivered one on a silver platter.

The world had suddenly transformed from a safe place to a deeply dangerous one without warning. He felt helpless. He thought about filleting fish the day earlier, the way the fish shook as he broke the skin with his knife. The smell of their roasting meat over the fire. No, the world hadn't transformed. Only their place in it had transformed. He wished he could reset time and undo every decision that had led to this trip.

Unexpectedly, a memory came to him of his father, who had driven an old beat up truck that routinely had issues. When he was little he had often ridden in the truck without a seat belt. In North Dakota, the seat belt requirement became law when Arthur had been much younger, around five, but North Dakotans were stubborn and hated change (especially change from big government). Even with the new law in place, no one had yet adopted wearing seat belts, and cops rarely ticketed for it. Arthur remembered riding with his dad one fateful day, leaning against the passenger door, staring out the window as his dad drove. He was blissfully daydreaming, unaware that anything bad could happen while in his father's presence.

Then, the stop light. They waited, and Arthur stared out his window, feeling the cold glass against his cheek, nearly falling asleep. He didn't notice the light turn green, only felt the vehicle moving, beginning its turn around the corner. The turn had been sharp, and fast, because that's how his father drove back then, back when Arthur was a little boy.

Unexpectedly, Arthur's door had flung open. It happened faster than Arthur could react. As the door opened, he began to fall out. Time stalled. He was falling toward the rolling asphalt as the truck turned the bend, watching as the street approached. He stopped breathing. He prepared for the pain, prepared for the sensation of the asphalt against his skin, possibly the car behind them rolling over his body.

Then, pressure on his wrist. His father holding his arm. Arthur had been caught at the wrist by his father at the last second. He remained there suspended as his father finished the turn. He remembered watching the street roll in a blur below him, hearing the rush of wind, the honking of cars. Then he was being pulled back into the truck, his father reaching across his lap to slam the door shut. Somehow, Arthur was alive, unscathed.

Later, his parents would learn that the passenger door latch had been faulty. Weight against it in just the right way would cause it to swing open, and they'd only been lucky up until that point. His parents, shocked at the close call, bought a new, more lightly used truck. Everyone started wearing seat belts.

Arthur had always wondered how his father, just before Arthur fell out that door, knew to reach out and grab his arm. How had he been so quick? Was it purely reflex? Had he heard the door open? Had he seen Arthur slipping out in his peripheral vision? He'd always assumed it to be simply that his father was an all-knowing god.

Arthur thought otherwise now as he felt the rush of adrenaline, that need to protect Jay at all costs. The door of the truck was opening, but it wasn't time to react just yet.

He looked at Jay and saw him start to shift. He was alive.

"You can leave whenever," the husk said. "I'm not sure you want to be here when... you know."

As Jay shifted in the roots, Arthur realized the boy would need more time. Arthur had to distract the husk. He had to ask questions, keep it talking.

"I will leave in a moment," Arthur said, "I... I guess I have some questions for you." He took a moment to continue thinking, his mind racing, not sure yet what to ask.

The husk seemed amused, its grin smug, "Sure, ask." Its voice created vibrations in the air as it spoke.

Arthur went with the first thing that came to his mind. "What exactly is a child to you?" Arthur asked.

The husk turned its head, stopped sharpening its stone tool. "What?" It asked.

"I mean, when did I become less appetizing to you? When did I become... not a child? I still feel like a child. I don't feel like I've ever really grown up."

The husk stared at Arthur, the light from the fire dancing across its dead, leathery skin. Its mouth was open, and Arthur could see its teeth, sharp like shark's teeth. Or rotten stubs, maybe, broken and chipped. It was hard to tell as the flames moved the light around its face.

Arthur continued, "My father passed away a few years ago. Stroke."

"That must have been very hard, you poor thing," the husk said.

Arthur ignored it, kept his eyes locked with the husk's. Arthur would eventually make a move, but now wasn't the time. At least it didn't feel like the time yet. They were building to something. He could feel it, his instincts screaming at him, adrenaline pumping rhythmically in his ears. Jay would live. Arthur may die, but Jay would live. He knew that to be true. Jay continued to shift in the roots, still trying to get out, but was doing so as still and as quietly as possible. The boy impressed him. Surely he was scared, as he had been when he'd heard the raccoon, but he was being brave. Arthur had told Jay to be quiet and stay still when near a threat, a threat like that very raccoon, and it seemed Jay had remembered.

"It was hard," Arthur agreed, "So I'm asking this because I've never felt like an adult, even after his death. I've lived in my father's shadow my entire life. My father was an impressive man. Did the right things at the right time. Knew how to handle conflict, could handle himself in a fight. I, clearly, cannot."

"No, you certainly cannot," the husk said.

"Even when I had my son, I still felt like nothing more than a child pretending to be a parent. So, can you tell me, when exactly did I become something more than just a child?"

In Arthur's peripheral, he saw Jay still shifting slightly, his hands behind his back, working against the roots. *Hurry*, he thought. Arthur was worried the husk would notice, would hear the child squirming. The husk smiled and Arthur tensed.

"You misunderstand our desire for their flesh," it said, going back to sharpening its knife. "When you order veal, why do you desire that cut of beef? A cutlet from a young cow? The meat's the most tender, the most pure, when the animal is still young. It isn't only sustenance, but an experience to be enjoyed, that is all. We prefer our meat young. It tastes a little fresher, a little less tainted.

"Enough talking. Have you decided? Will you stay to watch me clean the meal? I have a routine that I'm proud of. I leave some skin on the meat because it holds some of the moisture in. The skin curls as it roasts. Meat smoked over a campfire always tastes so good, wouldn't you agree?"

The fish meat in his stomach from last night wanted out, but Arthur refused. He was focused. He buried the sickness. His son needed to see strength. Jay was still working to free himself from the roots.

"You look angry," it said. "You can keep the head if you like. My treat. There's no good meat there. Something to remember your son by."

Arthur curled his fists. The husk was egging him on, he knew. Now wasn't the right time, but he wanted to break the husk, to teach it a lesson. The husk laughed, its dead skin stretching across its large skull as it did. Arthur took a step toward it. He'd die, he knew, but if words couldn't distract the thing longer, he hoped his death bought Jay some time. The husk matched his steps and too approached, now standing beside the fire, a hulking frame. It towered over him.

"Now, I know this is hard," it said, "This child is your flesh and blood. I get it. But the outcome won't change. It will only lead to wasted meat. Yours. Now would be a good time to go." A smile spread on its face, that leathery skin stretching again. "Go make more, then bring them, too," it said and laughed, an airy, hollow laugh.

Jay finally freed himself from the roots. Something shone in the boy's hands. The pocket knife, the knife Arthur had given him the night before. Before Arthur could make a move, Jay ran at the husk from behind, stabbing the knife into its leathery legs. The husk grunted, in shock or pain, Arthur did not know, but it was stunted regardless. Jay, sensing the moment, pulled the knife out, then stabbed again. Then again. The husk turned down to face Jay, its palm open.

Arthur saw it and felt it. The moment. The truck turned the corner and the door flung open. The husk reached his hand down to grab Jay, but Arthur was there first, his father's hand reaching out to grab onto the little boy and pull him back into the truck. For the first time in a long time, Arthur felt connected to his father again. The dry body of the husk slapped against Arthur like a dry sack of sand as they collided, but still the husk stumbled backward with the impact, Arthur holding strong onto its legs.

"Run, Jay! Go, now!" Arthur screamed.

Jay didn't run.

The husk was recovering, gathering its footing. Any second now, Arthur would be thrown or his neck would be snapped. He prepared himself, hoping Jay would find himself and run before he could watch it all happen. Arthur felt the husk's large hands grab his sides, felt it squeezing his waist. Crushed to death it would be, he realized. Not ideal, but so it goes. You don't get to choose your own death. "Run, Jay, dammit," he tried to say, but it came out breathless as he felt large palms squeezing his guts inward.

The husk grunted and the grip released. Arthur was dropped. His sides were screaming at him, but he ignored them. Jay had a stick from the fire in his hand and was thrusting it at the husk. The husk was stumbling now as the flames from the stick licked its dry skin.

As Arthur saw Jay wielding the stick, he remembered letting his son play with burning sticks whenever they made bonfires as a family, a cute little child playing with flaming weapons. Back then, he'd kept a watchful eye on his son as he poked and prodded the fire, speaking up when he thought the boy was doing something overly dangerous. Kris had questioned this, had thought they should instead scold the boy and keep him away from the fire entirely. It was unsafe, she'd said. But Arthur disagreed. He didn't really know why, but he was trusting his gut and his guidance and Kris let it go. He let Jay play, and taught him to be safe with fire instead of fearing it.

Now, the boy wielded the flaming stick as it was, a weapon against the husk, and Arthur knew he'd been right.

Arthur took the stick from his son, pushed the boy behind him. He stared at the husk, as it slapped at the fiery hole the boy had made in its body. Before the husk could recover, Arthur stuck the burning stick deep into the husk again, hearing the sizzling of dry, leathery skin. It went through without resistance. The husk howled, its screams rushes of wind that shook trees. The flames of the stick protruding from the husk died out, and Arthur rushed at the husk one last time, slamming into it with all his weight. The giant stumbled backward onto the ground. The forest shuddered with the impact, and the clearing erupted with gusts of wind.

Arthur took his son's hand and together they ran from the monster.

13

They ran through the woods as fast as Jay could. Jay led the way. Arthur checked the GPS map on his phone periodically to make sure they continued moving in the right direction. The wind was the strongest it had been since the night they'd gotten there, and they heard the Child Eater cursing them as they ran. Arthur didn't know if it was chasing, but knew they had to get out quickly.

"Child... Come back... Help me..." the wind said, and for once Arthur could hear it.

It couldn't chase them, Arthur realized. It wasn't mobile. It was stuck near its tomb for eternity, attracting prey with words as bait. Children were easy victims, attracted with simple suggestions, victims of their own naivety. In a predominately safe world, children didn't learn wariness until it was too late.

"Your father.... Lies.... I only... wanted to talk..."

Jay made no motion to stop, no hesitation, asked no questions. He wouldn't be tricked by the wind, by monsters, ever again.

"Child... Come back... Right now..."

"Fuck you!" Jay screamed.

"I will peel... Your meat from bone... And make you watch it cook."

"Ignore it, keep running," Arthur said quietly to his son.

The Child Eater's screams soon became breathless, sounding again like the soft brush of wind and nothing more.

When they jumped into the truck, not bothering with putting away the tent, the wind was but a subtle push against the vehicle. Arthur started the truck, put it into drive, and kept a strong grip on the steering wheel as they sped away. He glanced in the rearview mirror to make sure Jay had buckled. He had. The boy stared forward quietly as they drove, hands folded in his lap, alert but safe.

THE
TRANSFIGURATION

40

"There are many kinds of success in life worth having. It is exceedingly interesting and attractive to be a successful business man, or railway man, or farmer, or a successful lawyer or doctor; or a writer, or a President, or a ranchman, or the colonel of a fighting regiment, or to kill grizzly bears and lions. But for unflagging interest and enjoyment, a household of children, if things go reasonably well, certainly makes all other forms of success and achievement lose their importance by comparison." –Theodore Roosevelt

"I cannot make you understand. I cannot make anyone understand what is happening inside me. I cannot even explain it to myself." –Franz Kafka, The Metamorphosis

PΛRT I

1

Sam sat on the floor of his two studio apartment, staring at piles of cardboard boxes and wondering how in the world this had all happened. The boxes were artifacts of what would now become his *other* life, his *before* life, his *past* life, and he still didn't know exactly how he felt about it.

Well, that was a lie. He felt like shit; an empty pit behind his stomach was threatening to grow outward, cracking ribs and breaking skin like the alien bursting from Ripley's chest in *Alien 3*. Yes, he had an alien parasite growing inside his body, threatening to burst out of him if he didn't somehow kill it.

He didn't know how he'd do that, though. How does one exactly eliminate their feelings, when there are so many complex ones competing with each other? These feelings of emptiness and sadness were worthless feelings, feelings that would serve him no benefit, wouldn't get him to where he wanted to be. Yet he was prisoner to them, and they had him chained to the carpet of this grungy, cheap studio apartment. Fuck his feelings. He was just going to be happy. He could be as happy as he wanted to be. It was all a choice.

He didn't have any furniture yet in the new apartment. In his haste he'd taken only the essentials. A Pampers diapers box contained all of his office supplies: his work computer, his notebooks, his planner, his pens, an assortment of cables, and all the random garbage that had been left in the drawers that he hadn't had time to sift through. In a box he'd found in the garage for a baby swing were his two monitors and the monitor stand for a desk he no longer had (cheap desks were a dime a dozen, but one doesn't fuck around on good monitor arms). In his airport suitcase last used on a business trip a couple months back were his casual clothes: jeans, t-shirts, underwear and socks. In a tub that had once held Halloween costumes were the rest of his clothes, including his nice sweatshirts, his khakis, his dress shirts, and dress shoes for when he traveled. In a garbage bag was the collection of self-help and leadership books he'd pulled off the bookcase (knocking aside his wife's... ex-wife's... dirty dime-a-dozen romance novels), and another bag had his bathroom supplies. That was about it. It was all he had to his name now, because he'd given her everything. He wanted them to have everything, his family.

He sat on that carpet, smelling the old cat piss from the previous tenants leaking out of its fibers and leaching into his clothing, and really, really wondered how he'd gotten here.

He could have made a bigger stink of things (the house was in both their names, after all), could have taken at least half of what they owned. He would have taken their nice leather recliners and matching sofas, their 72 inch flat screen in the living room, their king size bed and padded bed frame, the walnut bookcases and matching walnut working station. He could have taken all of those things without much of a fight. He didn't think, at least. Maybe she would have taken him to court over everything. Yeah, she probably would have taken him to court. She definitely would have. Sam didn't like conflict much, so that wasn't an option.

What really stopped him, he liked to think, was his little girl. Little eight-year-old Dana. Dana, who Sam agreed would live with her mother, didn't need to see her home in disrepair. She didn't need to see the guy she'd called dad for the eight years of her life taking things away, things that made her home nice. No, that wasn't a responsible or kind thing for Sam to do at all. And Sam was very kind and very nice. Sam always buried his feelings and became a nice and good man. It made Sam feel happy about himself, that he did those things for them, let them keep his things like that. They were in a greater need of them then he was, especially now after the divorce.

He and his wife had made a choice, and it was an agreeable choice, he thought. It wasn't what he wanted, but he could accept it. Not now, but in time it would be easier. His wife would come around, wouldn't be so distant, and she'd let him see Dana at least once a week. Maybe she'd let him come home some day.

He found a garbage bag that had a few $20 plush blankets in it and tore it open. He pulled one out. It had been a blanket off the back of the couch, since he didn't want to steal the sheets and comforter from his wife. She needed a good night's sleep. Especially after the divorce. Things would be harder for her now. She had been a stay-at-home mom throughout their marriage, and now she was faced with having to re-enter the workforce. Money would be tighter for them for a while until she was able to sell the house. So let her keep those blankets, that warmth. Sam would make do. Sam made good money, and would be back on his feet soon enough.

Sam wrapped himself in the blanket, and it smelled so good. It smelled like home. There were perfumes in the fibers, a mix of their laundry detergents and sweat. It was a human stink that was pleasant because it was home. It was home. Eventually that smell would fade, and would take on a new smell after repeated washes. Eventually their smell, his family's smell, would fade, and only his would remain.

He laid down on the carpet, the cat stink wafting up around him in a plume. He wrapped the blanket tight around his head, enveloping him in their smell instead. If he closed his eyes, closed his thoughts, it still felt like he was with them, with his family, his old family. He loved them so much, and they loved him. Not like a father, not anymore, but once a family always a family. In a way.

He breathed in through his nose, feeling a tickle in his nostril. He breathed out and felt whatever had caused the sensation land on his lip. He opened his mouth to blow it away but it fell on his tongue. He lifted the covers away and took the small hair from his mouth.

It was a single dog hair.

Oh Riley, Sam thought to himself, Oh I'll sure miss that dog, too.

Sam fell asleep, reassuring himself that he wasn't procrastinating from setting up the apartment. No, he just needed a little nap was all, then he could unpack.

2

Sam awoke, his back sending sharp signals through his aching joints. Orange light filtered in from the closed window blinds. He found himself in a fetal position, nostrils burning from the pleasant aroma of the carpet. He tried to sit up but collapsed from sciatic jolts up his spine. He yelped quietly, rested flat on his back for a moment, then pushed up from the floor slowly with his arms.

He hadn't set up a clock yet and didn't know the time. He knew he had to work but wasn't overly concerned. A perk of working virtually, particularly once you've ascended the ranks a couple levels beyond peon, was that no one really paid attention to your time clock. Not that he had one, anyway. He was salaried. He worked when the job demanded he worked. Sometimes that meant eighty-hour work weeks. Sometimes that meant twenty.

Luckily work had been slow. His tasks had been reducing slowly as of late as he completed existing projects. For a time this concerned him, and he'd asked his boss for more work, some kind of goal or project that would keep his mind busy. No one at work knew what was going on at home, thankfully, and he didn't intend for them to find out. But he definitely needed something more to keep himself distracted. He enjoyed work, to an extent. It wasn't particularly fulfilling, but it was his job regardless, and the pay made up for any deficiencies he felt with his career progression.

He checked his phone to see when his first meeting was (since this tended to dictate the start of his day). Someone in India had dropped an invite on his calendar roughly an hour away, which was less than ideal. Either way, it was to be expected when working with a global company, a company with dedicated employees throughout the world, eager to make a name for themselves. Many of these employees lived for this job. Sam wasn't one to say that he lived for the company, but he did his part to stay afloat during the yearly round of reviews and fat-trimming. It was tough dealing with those on the other side of the spectrum, though, the people who seemed to think they were saving lives and treated every minor challenge as a world-ending event.

Sam decided he had enough time to wash the cat piss off his body. The smell seemed to have become embedded into his very skin. He hated cats. He'd have to call carpet cleaners when he found the time. Not that it really mattered. He'd be the only person to ever step foot in this apartment. He didn't plan to start dating again, and he certainly wouldn't bring Dana to this shit-hole.

He stood, found the bag with his clothing, and entered the bathroom. He forgot soap, realized he hadn't packed any, swore to himself, and decided to rinse himself off the best he could anyway. This decision proved poor when he turned off the flowing water and realized he didn't have any towels either as the cold air swarmed and tightened his exposed balls. He stepped out of the shower, shook his body as if he were a dog, and found the movement to be surprisingly efficient. He dressed, making a mental note of all the things he'd need to buy in between meetings that day.

In the other room he found his computer bag, pulled out his laptop, and sat down again on the carpet, leaning against the wall. He turned on the mobile hotspot setting of his phone, making another mental note to call about getting the internet set up. He pondered for a moment the many things within a home that people take for granted every day, such as chairs, food in the fridge, towels and internet. Creating a home takes time and hundreds of tiny little purchases to create the desired environment. And here he was, a forty-year-old man starting over from scratch.

The pain returned, the pain from the previous night that he'd buried since collapsing on the ripe carpet.

He shook it off. He didn't have time for any of that. It was going to be a good day. He was a good man and he was going to do good things today.

The laptop rang with the warning that a meeting was beginning. Sam didn't join yet. A lesson he'd learned long ago about unexpected meetings was that you had to set the tone and establish dominance. He wouldn't join until at least three minutes past the start of the meeting. He pulled up the meeting invite and read the notes, which said something about an inconsequential thing that was critically important to the business. He thought about making coffee, then added a coffee maker to his mental list of things he had to buy.

It was going to be a long day.

No, he corrected his thoughts, because thoughts became actions, It's going to be a good day. The start of something new and great.

After three minutes passed, he joined the call. There were several people waiting, three of them with their cameras on. He stared at them with their stupid faces, all smiling and eager to accomplish nothing of any significance. He really hated them all. No, he corrected his thoughts, because thoughts became actions. No, these people are my friends, and we're going to have a good day and I'm going to help them.

He turned on his own camera, smiling brightly from ear to ear.

"Sam," came a voice through the screen of his laptop, "We were beginning to worry you wouldn't make it."

They always said this, and it was always annoying to hear.

"Oh, you know me," Sam said, "Busy day bouncing between meetings. How are you? It's so good to see you guys again. Are you having a good day? Oh you know me. I'm always having a fantastic day. It's always a good day to be alive."

3

It was five in the afternoon, and Sam had spent the last two hours of his shift reminiscing about his home. He'd had an office that he loved, surrounded by bookshelves filled with books (only a fraction of which he'd actually read). He'd had an oak presidential desk with three large monitors, and a large flat screen television mounted on the wall for background noise. He deeply missed these luxuries after a day spent sitting on the floor with his small laptop screen.

It wasn't only the material luxuries that he was thinking about. It was stepping out of the office at lunch to eat with his wife (when she was home). It was listening to Dana burst in through the front door thirty minutes after three in the afternoon. It was the subtle static of living just beyond the office door that separated him from his world, from the things that truly mattered. The job was just a job, just a paycheck.

Now, in this apartment, there was nothing separating him from anybody. Sure, there were the walls that separated him from the other oddly quiet tenants. But those people weren't anybody important to Sam. They were just people, and as it was, his current world had no one of importance or value surrounding him.

But it was five now. His shift was over. In another life, maybe he stayed on for another hour or two in preparation for the next day or to get ahead on a project. Maybe he stayed late just to enjoy some time to himself. But now he had too much time to himself, and he realized just how easy it was to take for granted the most important things in his life. As the cliche goes, he didn't know what he had until it was gone.

He closed his laptop and set it on the ground. He pulled his phone from his pocket. It was still at a near full charge and was vacant of notifications. It was odd how phones could become physical representations of their owners. Social butterflies had phones beaming with energy: notifications, texts, calls, news alerts, etc. But people like Sam, people that had since been stripped of their identity, the phone was another representation of what it meant to be alone. He turned up the volume to make sure the ringer was still on, and it was. The phone was silent not because of an error on his part, but because no one wanted to talk to him.

He dialed his wife's number. "Wifey" appeared on the dialing screen. He'd have to change that eventually. At least until they got back together. Right then and there, however, it was too painful.

The dial went through five times before she answered.

"Sam? Why are you calling?" His wife asked.

"Hey, baby," Sam said.

"You can't call me that anymore."

"I'm sorry. You're right. It's habit."

There was silence on both sides of the phone as Sam waited for his wife to say something, taken aback by her harsh greeting, and she waited on him for unclear reasons.

"Well?" His wife asked, finally tired of the silence.

"I'm just calling to check in. It's quiet here. How's everything at the house? Good I hope. Is Dana getting settled in?"

"Sam, we're fine here. This isn't how a divorce works. Usually during a divorce we go our separate ways."

"Physically, maybe, but we can still be friends, right? We've spent half our lives together. Plus, we have a daughter to raise."

There was silence again on the other end.

"Are you there?" Sam asked.

"Yeah, why?" His wife responded.

"I don't know. Just expected you to say something."

"I don't have anything to say. Sam, I have to go. Is that all?"

"Well, no," Sam said, a hint of dejection in his voice. "I still wanted to talk to Dana for a bit. I'd like to talk to her every day so she doesn't forget about her father."

"Dana is busy right now," his wife said. More silence. There was the mumbling of words on the other end, but they didn't sound like Dana's or his wife's voice. She must have had her hand covering the receiver, or hugged the phone to her chest. Muffled words were sent back in return, this time from his wife's tone.

"I understand. When do you think she'll be free?" Sam asked. "And do you have visitors? Should I call back?"

"Maybe not today, Sam. Try again another time. Or better yet, I'll have Dana call you."

Sam tried to speak up before she hung up, to get an idea of when to expect the call, but the phone line had already been cut off. Sam felt brief, momentary anger at his wife's lack of kindness, but he quickly swallowed the emotion. That wasn't the way he wanted to live. He chose to be happy and see the best in people. She was busy was all. She'd call back eventually.

Sam smiled and laid his head against the wall.

Just a little rest, just for a bit, then he'd venture out into the world and get a few things he needed for his new home.

4

Sam had never really been sure why his wife had chosen to be with him, but figured most men (and maybe women, too) questioned why their partner held interest in them. Sam knew he had a poor image of himself. He tried to cover it up with what his wife called his toxic positivity. It's what kept all those dark thoughts behind enemy lines, all those secret and insistent negative thoughts. He'd done an excessive amount of counseling, and was open about it, so he knew all about keeping that dark passenger, that enemy of his id, locked up in a cage. He was in constant war with himself. Keep the emotions contained and he maintained power over his thoughts, behaviors, and actions.

Did his wife see that about him, the constant battle underneath it all? He didn't think she did.

"You can't be this happy all the time," she'd told him once while he was preparing dinner and talking optimistically about his day, glossing over the aspects of it that weren't pleasant.

He'd responded by insisting that it was good to be alive, that they were all lucky to be alive.

"Can't you complain about just one goddamn thing? Someone stole a parking spot from me today. They cut me off as I was about to pull in. I thought about that piece of shit all day. Does no one make you mad?"

Yes, people made him mad all the time, but he refused to give them any of his energy. "Baby doll," he'd said to her, and she cringed at his favorite nickname for her, "You have a choice. You can be angry, or you can be happy that you gave that person a good parking spot. Maybe they were having a bad day."

She'd thrown her hands up in frustration. "You're impossible," she'd said, "No, it wasn't a good thing. The person was an asshole and I just want you to agree with me that they were assholes. Just complain about something. Anything."

But he had nothing on his mind that he'd give negative energy. The world was a good place. The world was a happy place. He was privileged to be living in it.

"Sometimes I worry there's something wrong with you," she'd said to him before leaving the room, "No one is this happy all the time." And then she'd said the words that haunted him still to this day, because he felt it, too, underneath the careful facade he'd built that was his identity. "Sometimes you scare me."

He often wondered if he should give in, should give her what she wanted. Maybe it wouldn't hurt to complain a little bit, to let a little of the evil into his present mind. But he cast those thoughts with a shake of the head, returning to the careful slicing of carrots for a stew they'd have for dinner. No, he couldn't let the evil in. The evil would poison his mind. He had to stay vigilant, stay positive. The darkness could corrupt anyone that gives it power.

But still, he would secretly wonder sometimes. Was she right? Was there something wrong with him?

PART II

5

Sam stood outside his home, wrapped in a thick coat with the hood up. He was across the street behind a tree, watching his family from the living room window. It was late at night on a weekend, and it seemed Dana was being allowed to stay up late to watch a movie. It hurt to not be there with them, watching that movie, whatever it was. He couldn't see the screen from the angle of view that he had.

Yet what hurt the most wasn't the two of them, but the man that sandwiched his wife and daughter.

Sam had tried calling every day for the last few weeks, but each time he was told Dana was busy. A few times he'd heard muffled voices, and now he knew why. His wife was moving on. Perhaps she'd moved on long before the marriage had ended.

As he stood there, he found himself running scenes in his mind, remembering the months before she confronted him to tell him she was unhappy. His wife had always been a little distant. She wasn't one to be particularly warm or affectionate, but there were still small signs. Three months before "the talk", she'd stopped talking to him on the phone unless he was the one to call first. Her wedding ring came off six months before that because "she was gaining weight and it no longer fit her finger". He couldn't remember the last time she'd told him she loved him.

Those little things hadn't bothered him at the moment. At the time, it seemed to him that his marriage was simply maturing. People get more comfortable over time, after all, and it wasn't something to be worried about.

Now, however, he could see the truth. She'd been drifting away from him under his nose, and he'd been too stupid to see it.

His counselor's voice appeared in his mind, telling him that he wasn't a mind reader, that he couldn't manage someone else's emotions, that he was only in control of himself. He heard this reminder and tried to shift his negative thoughts to positive ones. They hadn't drifted apart. They'd learned more about themselves, which happened to mean they weren't meant to be together, and that was okay. His wife... ex-wife, had found someone that was possibly a better match for her. That was a good thing. She'd be happier now. Good for her.

Dana was laughing at the movie, sandwiched between her mother and new father. Even his little girl was happy. This made him sad, but he knew the sadness was selfish and self-absorbed. Good for them. Let them enjoy their time together. Life is good.

At their feet lay Riley, the golden retriever. He felt a surge of jealousy for the dog. It did nothing but love and make messes, but still it was allowed in the house. Dogs loved unconditionally, and in return were either tolerated or loved in return. Expectations for dogs were low.

Tears in his eyes, Sam forced himself to turn away and walk back to his car, parked several blocks away.

6

His dreams were becoming a prison, but he wanted to sleep because the real world was unbearable. Sleeping helped him forget, if only for a little bit. Sometimes the dreams had him strapped to a chair. Sometimes in his dreams he faced memories.

He dreamt of his father, a short, fat, balding man that was in his life until the age of sixteen. He didn't know much about his father, and his father didn't know much about him. His father didn't care to spend any time at all with Sam, and seemed to show up at home solely to fuck his mother and watch television.

Even so, Sam loved his father, as young boys do, and he'd vied for his attention whenever he saw him. His father would speak to him kindly, never harshly, but his tone was dismissive. When he asked to play cars with him, his father would say "Yeah, buddy, sometime, okay?" And Sam would walk away, back to his room, back to being alone.

As he dreamed and reflected, he wondered why he'd kept trying. Surely he knew the answer that would come, the feeling of disappointment and inadequacy to follow. Why did he keep trying to get love from a man that had no more love to give?

In other dreams he reminisced on old girlfriends, both short and serious. He'd never been one to end an engagement, always being on the receiving end. There was never a reason, only a slow drip drip drip as the valve of affection was turned off and people stepped away. Sometimes kindly, saying they simply weren't a match for each other. Other times the separation was less than ideal. He dreamt a couple times of the worst one, where his partner had slept with his best friend several times without him knowing. When he found out, he'd learned that many of his friends knew about it, that it had been going on and no one had chosen to tell him. This had enhanced the feelings of betrayal. In his naive youth, he'd given her another chance because she promised it wouldn't happen again. After Sam forgave her twice more for similar betrayals, she simply moved on and never spoke to him again.

Sam dreamed often of his daughter, too, who he dearly missed spending time with. Why hadn't she told her mother to let her come visit him? Had his daughter moved on from him, too?

Was he simply not good enough for anyone?

How were people so good at severing connections to people that should mean something more to them? Why couldn't Sam similarly disengage with such ease?

The dreams that weren't nightmares were often ones of his dog, tied to his leash but wagging his tail, still eager to see Sam. It seemed dogs didn't discard as easily as humans did. Sam wondered sometimes if he were more canine than human.

7

Sam answered the call from his laptop and was greeted by his manager's smiling face. "Hello, Sam. I'd say it's good to see you, but you joined with your camera off."

Sam found the activation of the camera odd in this case. His boss rarely used his camera for their weekly private sessions.

He brushed back his hair, checked his shirt, sat against a wall (he still didn't have a chair), and turned on his camera.

"Welcome," his boss said. "It's good to see you. Truly. It's been how long since we've last seen each other?"

Sam had to think about this. He used to travel frequently to business summits that had flimsy justification for existing outside of an excuse for virtual employees to travel the world. However, whether due to budget or other reasons, travel had been slow lately. "Was it our site visit back, oh, last year in India?" He asked.

His boss nodded his head, his close cut hair gelled so stiffly the hairs didn't move. "Yes, I think it may have been that. What a fun trip that was."

Sam nodded his head and smiled. "Yes, our Associates in India were great guests. I can't say I enjoyed the food, though. The thought of it still gives me heartburn. Such culture there, though. If only they'd tuned down their spiciness for us."

His boss laughed at that, which was then followed by silence. These calls could quite often be awkward, especially when there was little on the agenda to discuss. However, they were mandated by company policy to check in weekly. It benefited the employee, the company policy read, to have frequent check-ins with management.

"Listen. Sam. This meeting will be a little bit different. I'm going to invite someone on the call, and then we'll get into the agenda I have prepared. Did you have anything for me?"

Sam thought for a moment obligatorily, then said, "No, nothing from me."

"Okay, let me grab our guest. He'll join shortly."

A few seconds of more silence passed as Sam considered who might join. This wasn't uncommon. Not really. If he was working a project, sometimes his boss would bend the policy slightly and invite another co-worker on the call to discuss the project. But Sam didn't have a major project at the moment, and hadn't had one in some time.

There was a chime as the person joined, and Sam recognized the name immediately. The Human Resources representative didn't turn on their camera.

"Okay Sam. This is going to be hard for me, but as you know, your work lately has been slipping into the realm of unsatisfactory. You've always been a quiet, dependable person, but lately you've been missing assignments and lacking motivation in your recent tasks. You've been neglecting your business duties in this regard, so we will be letting you go today."

There was silence again as Sam processed the news. Sure, he'd taken more days off than usual, but he was salaried and he got his required work done. He hadn't been assigned any major projects. It must have been a misunderstanding.

"Do you have any questions for us, Sam?" His boss asked.

There was ringing in his ears. Sam felt as if he were in shock. He'd given everything to this job, to his family, and now it seemed he was losing both. No, he couldn't lose either. It didn't make any sense at all. He was a good husband. He was a good father. He was a good employee. He was satisfactory.

"Sam?"

"Yes, I'm sorry, I'm here."

"Do you have any questions? This mustn't come as a surprise. We've been having these talks for weeks now."

This was a lie, of course. His boss was covering his tracks. It was required that employees have previous documented infractions prior to termination. It was policy. Sam and his boss hadn't had any such conversations. Yet, it was his word against his boss's, and certainly his boss would have ensured there was proper documentation before proceeding.

"Sir, my apologies here, I don't question your judgment in the slightest, but is it possible there was a mistake? I believe that I've been maintaining my responsibilities to the corporation and to the projects I've been assigned."

"Therein lies the challenge, Sam, as we've been discussing. You haven't been working on any projects for quite some time now. As a member of this company in your standing, it's expected that you use your time wisely to the benefit of the company, and if projects aren't assigned to you, for you to find initiatives that provide benefit."

Checkmate, Sam realized. He'd been set up for this, for failure. For what reason he didn't know. It was possible his boss simply wanted fresh blood on his team, and Sam was the odd man out. There was nothing he could do here. "I understand," he said, knowing there was nothing he could say to change the situation otherwise. "Is there a severance package?"

"Of course," his boss said, "You've been a valued member of this team for over a decade. You'll be given three months salaried severance, starting this month. You will log off your computer following this meeting, and we will send you a package in the mail for you to ship back your computer in the coming days."

"Okay," Sam said, not knowing what else to say or ask. "Okay."

"Any other questions, Sam?"

"No, sir."

"Okay. Thank you for your time with us. I've enjoyed working with you."

"I've enjoyed working with you, sir. Thank you."

The call ended, and Sam did as he was commanded. He shut down the computer.

"Shit!" He exclaimed suddenly in the silence. He'd forgotten to tell his boss that he had a change of address. It didn't matter. He'd send him a text. For a while he sat there, thinking, processing. Then he dug out his personal computer, intending to dust off his resume. This would all work out, he told himself. Everything would be okay. Everything is always okay.

8

He was doing laps around his studio apartment because he didn't want to leave. He wasn't sure why he didn't want to leave. He simply didn't feel like it, even though he had nothing to do. His apartment was starting to take some shape at least. He had furniture now, and he'd put up his motivation posters. A poster with a book resting on a table said "Learn as if you will live forever, live like you will die tomorrow", and another beside it with a mountain top as its backdrop said, "Give good thought to the happiness that you give out."

He checked the time. It was too early. He did a few more laps, finding himself getting sweaty in the process. After this he'd have to shower and change. It was good to remain clean and fresh, even when alone in your own home.

He took out his phone and dialed his wife. She would answer this time. Yes, she would.

Six rings played out over the phone's speaker.

She didn't answer.

How long had it been seen he'd spoken to his family? To his daughter? A brief thought of involving the courts crossed his mind, to at least gain legal right to see his daughter again, but it was only a passing consideration. He trusted his wife. She was a good person going through a hard time, as was he. Attacking this situation with anger would only make things worse.

He just missed both of them so much that it hurt. He missed his home.

He missed his dog, his Riley. Riley would keep his feet warm during his daily meetings, always present for a surprise cuddle.

The silence of the apartment was becoming deafening.

Would Riley still love him unconditionally, even if the rest of his family was in the process of moving on from him? Sam thought that he would. Dogs didn't understand the concept of abandonment. In many ways, dogs were more human than human beings. At least, that's what Sam thought.

9

It was late in the night, and Sam stood outside his home again, watching through the window. Every once in a while he'd see either his wife pass by or his daughter. Once he'd seen the man that had replaced him. No, was borrowing his family he corrected himself. They were all going through a rough time was all.

But he wasn't here for them this time.

He was there for Riley.

The front door opened, the screen door creaking. They were late tonight. They would have let Riley outside and fed him at least an hour earlier. It was inconsiderate to treat such a loving animal with such a lack of grace.

The screen door swung shut with a crack through the silent night, and Riley began to ravage his bowl of processed food bits. When the dog was finished, it licked the bowl clean, then ventured out into the lawn, careful not to stretch its chain too tight. It found a spot, circled it, and relieved itself.

It seemed unfair for such a beautiful and loyal creature to have to complete its basic needs outside the family home, yet again another disrespectful gesture. Sam was disappointed in his family. At least he would have sat beside Riley just outside the door and kept him company. Most nights, at least. Because he truly loved the animal. No, not an animal. Family member.

Without thinking, Sam began to approach the dog, eager for its embrace. It had been so long since he'd embraced a member of his family, and this one in particular he missed the most. He wanted to feel the dog's warmth against him, its fur tickling his skin, its dog scent creeping into his nostrils.

Riley sensed him coming and stood alert. Sam stopped walking and started questioning his actions. Would the dog bark and expose him? Could this lead to a restraining order of sorts and forever lock him away from his family? He prepared himself for running away.

But the dog didn't bark, only began wagging its tail and eagerly approaching him, head lowered in a sign of obedience. Sam understood and approached, slowly at first, then much more quickly. He embraced the dog in a hug, and the dog buried its nose into Sam's chest. The dog was shaking back and forth, thrust side to side by the power of its excited tail, and Sam felt the same energy as the two came together again.

This was unconditional love. Dogs always had unconditional love for their owners. Dogs never turned a blind eye to their family.

Before he knew it, Sam was crying. He was crying as he nuzzled his face deep into the fur of familiarity and happiness and wholesomeness.

"I love you, Riley," Sam said, and the dog seemed to whine in agreement.

Then a thought came to Sam. He looked up at the house. There was movement in the living room, but the lights were off. He couldn't see who it was, but was worried it was his wife. She would see him out there in the lawn. Optimism swarmed within him, a sensation created from the act of once again being loved. He could go to her, his wife, and she would welcome him home. Like Riley, being with Sam again would create that surge of desire that brought lovers together after conflict.

He was about to stand when the reflection revealed the person behind the shadow. It was a man, the man that had been there on earlier nights, sitting in his place on the couch and watching television in his home with his wife and daughter. His replacement. His wife's upgrade.

No, he knew then. No only dog's loved unconditionally.

"Riley," he whispered to the dog, as the man crossed through the living room, walking toward the entry way and the door, likely to retrieve the pet that had been chained up outside. "Riley, do you want to come home?" He asked, because home was where your family was, and again the dog whined.

He had to think quickly, and he had to trust the dog, before the man opened the door. He found Riley's collar, unclipped the chain, and Riley was released.

"Follow me, Riley," he said, and then he left it up to fate.

He stood and he ran, trying to remain in the shadows. Behind him he heard the screen door creak open, heard a voice calling for the dog behind him, but he didn't look back. He ran alongside the street now, back to his car. He could still hear the man, far back there, calling the pet back. He hoped Riley had chosen him, hoped for once someone would choose him and only him.

He reached his car panting, three blocks away. He could hear the man far back by his old home, calling for the animal. His voice was becoming louder now, more insistent.

But the dog wasn't there for him to find. Riley was with him. Riley had chosen well, had followed his family. Sam knelt down to the eager animal wagging its tail and embraced it again. "Oh thank you, Riley," he said, "Thank you, thank you, thank you."

He opened his car door and the dog jumped inside.

10

Sam dreamt of himself as a child, sitting against the flag post at school as the other children played on the playground equipment. Sam sat reading a book, keeping to himself, because he'd never been very social. He'd always been a happy and kind child, but relationships scared him. Kids tended to reject him.

But he did have one friend. Daniel, Danny for short. He didn't play with Danny often. Usually only at his home when he came over to stay the night for a sleepover. They'd play pretend games with Sam's toys, would sometimes invent games and play with play doh. Danny was a good friend.

But Danny was only his friend when they weren't at school, because Sam was weird.

A group of kids approached Sam, still sitting there reading his book. Danny was with them.

"Look at this weirdo," one of the kids said, a bully, a kid Sam didn't even remember the name of because bullies were so numerous. "Watcha readin'?" The kid asked.

Sam didn't answer. He ignored the kid, because sometimes that was best. A part of him, somewhere deep within his mind, told him to stand his ground, to metaphorically puff out his chest. But Sam didn't really know how to do that. Sam was happy and kind and honest and genuine. Sam saw the best in people, and hoped for goodness even when he knew there was none left.

The kids around the bully, the bully-lites, laughed, and Sam made eye contact with Danny. He didn't beg Danny to help him with what was to come, but his eyes surely told a story, a story where his friend needed his help. But Danny was role playing, and Sam was only his friend when it was convenient for Danny. Danny was human. Danny wasn't loyal.

"What, don't you talk?" The bully-supreme asked, and Sam said nothing. His only thoughts now were on how bad this would get. How long would they be there, picking on him, before they got bored and walked away? Would he have to protect himself again?

"Hey, I'm talking to you," the bully said, and started to kick his shoe. Sam didn't like that, but still said nothing, and instead pretended to keep reading his book. They would get bored and walk away, he knew. Eventually. Even Danny.

"Whatever," the bully said, and the group carried on, leaving Sam there by the flag post. Danny didn't even look back. Sam was hurt, but if he was honest, he understood. Danny just wanted to maintain his relationship with his friends, all his friends. That was okay. Sam continued to read his book, but there was a hurt in his heart that took some time to go away.

Danny wanted to hang out that weekend, maybe stay up and watch some movies. Sam eagerly agreed.

11

"Do you have my dog?" She asked.

"No, I don't have our dog," he said, "He stayed home, remember?"

"Don't be coy. You know the dog was to stay with us as part of the agreement," she said, "Dana is worried about the dog. If you have it, you're causing harm to your daughter."

"I don't have the dog," he said. I am the dog, he thought, and almost laughed to himself. Was he losing his mind? "Can I talk to Dana? Maybe I can reassure her that everything is fine."

"Dana is at school."

"No she's not. It's an early out. Last Friday of every month is always an early out."

"Not this month, Sam. She's in school. You can't talk to her."

"Will you ever let me talk to her?" He wasn't sure if he was begging, or if it was a simple question.

"Sam, we're not talking about this right now," his wife said, "We're talking about the dog."

"The dog's name is Riley," Sam said defiantly, and the dog jumped up from the hasty bed he'd made of blankets in a corner of the apartment. It lowered its head as it neared Sam, ready to accept a scratch on the head. Sam eagerly abided. If the dog barked, they'd both be in trouble, but he knew it wouldn't. Riley was loyal. Dogs were loyal. Riley would never betray him.

"Sure. Riley is a damn dog. A damn dog that, if you have, is property that must be returned home."

"Do you see Dana as property?" Sam asked, somewhat shocked by his own words.

There was silence for a time on the other end. His wife didn't take the bait. "If you have the damn dog, Sam, I will call the police and have him returned. And you'll never speak to Dana again."

The line disconnected.

You'll never speak to Dana again.

The line felt ominous. It wasn't only a threat, it was the blatant truth, now out in the open. He knew he wouldn't take her to court, though. Neither of them wanted that for Dana, to go through that. Even so, could he win a court case? He had a studio apartment and no job. He had nothing to his name. He'd let his wife have everything in some foolish attempt to garner some last minute favor, to try to win her back by offering her the space she requested.

No, it was more than that, he reminded himself. He didn't want Dana to go through painful change. If he was to be the only thing removed from the equation, for Dana's sake, he was okay with that. Thinking from Dana's perspective, he could live with that. From his perspective, he was barely alive. He was a cockroach squashed beneath his wife's heel.

Could he blame her though?

He shook the thought from his mind. There was nothing wrong with him. There was nothing wrong with him.

Riley barked, pulling him from his thoughts. He realized that he was crying. He embraced the dog tightly, so tightly he was momentarily fearful he might choke the dog to death.

PART III

12

Sam felt alive because Riley was alive. They chased each other around the apartment laughing. Bills were piling up and Sam had stopped applying for new jobs, but it didn't matter. Sam had his dog back, and his dog had him. They were two peas in a pod, as the cliche went. Hell, they were practically the same pea in the same pod.

13

Sitting on the floor of his apartment, which now smelt pleasantly like a dog's aroma as the cat piss had been overtaken by Riley's presence, he cuddled with the dog. He breathed in the dog's essence as they lay there, near sleep, his face buried deep within the dog's thick, curly hair.

He thought about how he'd been disposable, but Riley was not. Dogs were, usually, permanent fixtures for families. They pooped and pissed all over the house, but the owners dutifully cleaned the mess and didn't question it. The worst a dog faced was a scolding, but it rarely got kicked out. Dogs loved their owners unconditionally, and generally, the unconditional love was returned by the owners.

Sam wished that's what he could be to someone out there in the lonely world, a man loved unconditionally, forever and ever until he died.

Sam wished he was a dog.

14

"How many times did you come over here and spy on us, you sicko?" His wife asked. "You're unhinged. You're unsafe. You have issues, hiding behind a facade of kindness. Do you know that? That's why I kicked you out. You're dangerous."

Sam said nothing, listening to the barrage, wondering why he'd answered the phone.

"The police have a warrant, you know. You have stolen property. That's a crime. And we have eye witnesses. You're going to go to prison."

"Can I talk to Dana?" Sam asked.

His wife guffawed. "You're a real piece of work. Do you know how much she's crying, so scared for Riley?"

"I told you I don't have the dog."

"Why are you doing this?" His wife asked.

I just want to come home, He thought, but didn't say. He was aware now that things were beyond repair. There was no going home. "I'm not doing anything. I just want to speak to my daughter. Does she ask about me?"

"Not even once," his wife answered, the tendrils of hatred curling out of the phone as she spoke. Sam felt like throwing up. "They're going to be there soon, Sam. Give them the damn dog and move on."

"Why are you doing this?" Sam asked.

"What? Me? Why are you doing this? What is wrong with you?"

The line went dead.

15

The police came for the dog two days later, two soft knocks on the door. They spoke his full name, stepped in the apartment, searched and asked their questions. They left without a dog, because there was no dog. There was only a man alone in his apartment.

16

But the man wasn't a man for much longer. Soon he found that it was easier walking around the apartment on four legs instead of two. It was awkward at first, as if his body wasn't accustomed to being hunched over, and his neck was getting severe cramps from leaning back to look up as opposed to straight ahead. But Sam saw these things as necessary as part of his transition from Sam to Riley, or rather the binding of the two together as one, his metamorphosis into a more beautiful being than he had been before.

In the first few days after his transition, he found it hard to walk on both his front and back legs. His back legs were longer than his front legs, and so walking felt unbalanced with his awkward human frame. Yet over time, he adjusted, and found that bending his back legs slightly leveled his back to allow for a comfortable walk. It also gave him leverage to spring forward quickly if he chose to do so. His neck also soon grew accustomed to its new angle, as if his muscles were strengthening as he took on his canine form.

He also dealt with a nasty habit for his front paws to spread back out into their human digits. He had to consciously focus to force those uncomfortable digits back into a singular paw, one more accustomed for travel than for grabbing. This was the hardest human habit to break, and took the longest to overcome.

Before his transformation, he had tied a rope to any appliance requiring use, such as the fridge. He could now swiftly open the fridge with a bite, though those weak human muscles too took time to strengthen. Now, however, he found he could pull open the door and feed himself with ease. He was also becoming less concerned about what he was eating, and would simply eat whatever he found in the fridge (even spoiled). He also found the toilet to be an unlimited supply of water, which tasted just fine to his dog senses.

He liked it better this way. He didn't need furniture or other human comforts, because he could sleep and eat right from the floor. He roamed the apartment, barking and enjoying a simpler life. He found he could keep himself entertained simply by running laps around his apartment, though sometimes his neighbors would pound on the walls if he were running at odd hours. He didn't care. Sometimes he'd bark back at them.

He found he did miss his family, though. He longed for scratches from his owners. Not cuddles or extended periods together, just an acknowledgment of his presence. He wanted to see them, receive their love, and then proceed doing dog things.

He decided it was time to go home.

17

He pulled the rope to open his apartment early that night after sundown, straining to get the heavy door open, having to tug back several times until the stubborn thing finally relented. Then he was free, running through the halls of the apartment complex until he reached the entry. Here he met his first challenge: he hadn't been able to tie a rope to this door while he'd still been human, and had no way to open it.

He sat on his hind legs and patiently waited for someone to open the door for him.

When someone did finally come what must have been hours later (time processed differently for a dog, and Sam wasn't accustomed to that just yet), it was two drunk humans. They scanned the double doors open with a beep, and pulled open the gateway to freedom. They didn't see Sam crouched there until they stepped inside.

"Jesus Christ," said the first.

"What the fuck, man," said the second. They both recoiled from him. Hadn't they seen a dog before? Sam wondered as he ran out of the opening. He didn't think about it again either way, because he was on his way to his family, his humans that would love him unconditionally.

It was a long run, and Sam got lost a few times, having to backtrack and gather his bearings again. It was tougher navigating as a dog, only able to locate by scent and sight alone. He missed being able to read street signs (his vision was starting to fail him in his new state, words becoming illegible, certain objects blurry and seemingly out of focus, colors duller), but he could sense more through his nose, the world more lively in that way.

Eventually he found his way home, though it was much, much later now. He didn't know this for sure, but he could sense it, from the deep darkness of the night and from the intense silence that was normal during the latest hours.

He prodded up to the doorway and sat there on his hind legs. There was no way for him to get inside, unable to open the door with his new paws. It was likely locked anyway. He first thought he might sleep here that night, wait for his family to wake and find him there in the morning, excited and happy to have their pet home.

Instead a new idea came to him, and he sprinted into the back yard, the morning dew soaking into his paws and cold to the touch. When he came to the fence, he jumped up and over it, using his back legs to thrust himself over the top. Dogs could jump much higher than humans, after all. In the backyard he approached the back door, and at the bottom of it, the doggy door. Would they have left it unlocked, hopeful Riley would return to them?

He pushed his head against the door, but found no such luck. The door was locked and refused to swing inward. He tried to think about other options, but it was harder with his dog brain. So he did the first thing that came to mind: He rammed into the doggy door with his shoulder. On the third strike, he felt the door crack and bend slightly, so he continued to slam the full weight of his body against the door.

He didn't realize how loud the act was until the lights in the house turned on. There were voices inside, but he couldn't understand what they were saying. The words were sounds only. Some deep, some high.

The door opened, and before him stood the man and his wife. Behind them, he could see Dana, perfect Dana, his beautiful Dana.

"Oh my God," said the man, putting his arm in front of his wife as if to protect her. It wasn't the reaction Sam expected. He expected instant love at the return of their dog.

"Jesus, is that you, Sam?" Asked his wife. She backed away from the man, deeper into the room behind them. "I think I'm going to be sick," she said, grabbing Dana as she walked. "Dana, come with me?"

"What is it mommy?" Dana asked, and her voice was like a soft blanket wrapped around Sam's battered heart.

Sam prodded past the man, who attempted to grab at him but missed. Dogs were more agile than humans and tend to be slippery. He barked in excitement to finally see her, his daughter, the beaming light at the end of his endlessly dark tunnel.

Dana screamed. She hid behind her mother and started to cry, eyes closed, still screaming. The sound was piercing to Sam's delicate dog hearing. It stopped him in his tracks and he stared at the girl.

"Do something!" His wife yelled at the man that had replaced him.

Sam didn't move, didn't care to move. He was in shock. He expected little Dana to come running to him, to hug her long lost pet. Instead she recoiled from him. All of his family stood before him, recoiling in fear. There was no love here.

Sam turned to run. He didn't know where, but he needed to run. He needed to get away. The pain was too great. He was their pet, yet they still rejected him. It was all wrong.

But that was emotional pain, and as he turned, he saw the stick being swung as a weapon, and had seconds to process that it was the closet rod used to hang jackets. The man somehow had torn it off the wall, the jackets lying in a heap on the ground, spilling out of the closet.

Thwunk was the sound that rang out as the rod connected with his face, and he crumpled to the floor, knowing physical pain now, too. No, he wanted to say, No, we don't do this to family. I'm not an intruder. I'm your dad, I'm your husband, I'm your loyal protector. I'm Riley. Don't you remember me? Don't you love me? But it didn't matter. He felt the impact on the top of his head, and the world around him started to go dark as he fell asleep for the last time.

18

What lay before the family, broken and bleeding, was an amalgam of man and canine parts. The family dog butchered, skinned, and worn by Sam like clothing, the parts of the dog stretched to their limits as Sam had squeezed inside them. On his head was a mask made of Riley's face, with the eyes cut out so he could see. Without the jaw bone of a real dog, the mouth of the mask lay flat grotesquely against the chin of the mask. Around his body was Riley's own body, worn like a jacket and loosely sown at the front to prevent it from falling off. The arms of the dog had been kept whole outside of the ends, where the paws had been removed so as the rest of Sam's arm could be squeezed through. What remained of Riley from the waist down was a set of shorts that ended before Sam's knees, the skin there already shredding at the ends from over-stretching. Dried blood caked the inside of the Riley-suit, and dry flecks rubbed off on the floor where Sam now lay.

Sam's wife held her daughter close, shielding her eyes as her daughter continued to scream. When the screams stopped, she sobbed, asking "Is that daddy? Is that Riley? Mom, what is that?" As her mother shushed her quietly against her breast.

"It's okay, darling," her mother said to her as she stroked her hair. "Everything is okay now."

"Jesus," said the man holding the rod that had killed Sam, "You weren't kidding. The man was nuts."

"You should call the police," Sam's wife said. "I'm going to get Dana out of here. We're never coming back here. We're selling this home and buying something somewhere far away."

"What about me?" Asked the man.

"You're welcome to come with us, if you like," Sam's wife said.

"Did he have a life insurance plan?" The man asked. "I wonder if we could get something out of this."

"You'll be lucky to escape some jail time if you don't call 911 and start acting terrified about what you've done," Sam's wife said, still holding her daughter's face tight to her chest.

Sam's wife walked her daughter to a table in the entryway, grabbed her purse and car keys, and stepped around Sam out the back door. "Call the police," she said, "And call me later."

Sam's wife gave the man a kiss on the lips and then left, taking Dana far away from the man that had killed their dog.

OUR GREATEST ENEMY

50

"His father watched him across the gulf of years and pathos which always divide a father from his son." –John Marquand

"If the past cannot teach the present, and the father cannot teach the son, then history need not have bothered to go on, and the world has wasted a great deal of time." –Russell Hoban

1

Adam sped away from his home town of Colorado Springs on his way to Pike's Peak. In his passenger's seat was a backpack with several days worth of snacks and water he'd purchased less than half an hour ago. It was plenty more than he expected needing, but however long it took, he would stay on the mountain until the end. He knew exactly where he wanted to be when it all ended, had thought about it often over the last few months.

A news alert, the catalyst for this sudden trip, had flashed across his phone a little over an hour ago. He'd left work without telling anyone where he was going. On his way out of the building, he'd been surprised to find that few others were in any sort of concern. It seemed like just another day, as if nothing was happening. Perhaps others didn't know what it all meant, where it would all lead. Perhaps people had decided the only option was to continue doing what they'd done their entire lives, as if the end of the world and staying at work weren't all that much different anyway. Perhaps they were in ignorance that anything could happen, that the government would take care of them. Adam wasn't as optimistic. Luck always, inevitably, ran out.

While he drove he called his sons. They both lived hundreds of miles away, too far to reach in person before everything happened, so a call was the best he could do. He told them he loved them, that he was proud of them. He explained that he was disappointed they'd grown distant after so many years, but that his feelings for them had never changed. He'd accepted that these things happened. It was only natural. As children discover themselves, they find that their passions didn't always align with their parents and they moved on. His oldest moved to the tech center of the world in California and worked for a start-up company that Adam didn't really understand, and the other found a way to make a meager living in Florida, intent on spending the rest of his life in the sun and along the coast. Adam, who had spent his whole life in one state, long ago decided to stay where he'd always been, and where his wife was buried.

He'd briefly considered going to his wife's grave after he'd left the office, but it was only a passing thought. His wife was not there. Buried there was only her body, the gravestone a marker to spark memories and create the sensation that they could still speak to each other. But over the years since her death, he'd learned he didn't need that gravestone. He could talk to her wherever and whenever he wanted. He could summon her at will and remember her. He could hold conversations with her in the quiet of his empty home. Life was all perception. Life was magic, really. People were equipped to do just about anything they wanted, could create any scenario simply by closing their eyes. He'd talked to his wife many times since her passing, and he refused to conjure her in these last moments. He loved her, he missed her, but she was at peace. She didn't deserve to see the imminent chaos ahead.

He arrived at the entrance of Pike's Peak and paid for his ticket, $15, both surprised and not surprised that there were still people manning the entrance. He didn't know when exactly things would happen, but he was prepared for them to happen soon, or within a couple days at the latest. Ordinary life didn't move at a breakneck pace. Not really. Life felt fast paced, but things never changed quickly. Change happened slowly, unnoticed over many years, so slowly that a person would find themselves reflecting back and wondering where and when it had all gone.

As he drove the twists and turns up the mountain, he took in the scenery. The snow-tipped mountain tops surrounding the red-colored rock underneath. The red and brown hills and mounds that scattered the ground below. He rolled down his window and breathed in the clean air. It was thinner as he went up, tasted crisper, untainted. The world was such a beautiful place, for a few more moments at least. He was glad he'd chosen this spot.

When he reached the top of the mountain he found no other vehicles. Tourism was slow early on a weekday, he figured. He parked the vehicle in a designated spot, got out, and began walking without clear direction. There was a platform and fenced off areas for tourists to take pictures, but it didn't feel like the right place to camp out. He wanted somewhere comfortable to lie down and watch, somewhere with a good view to watch the sky. He wandered around, going off the defined path, until he found his father sitting on the edge of a flat rock waiting for him. He was staring out at Colorado Springs far below them. He didn't expect his father to beat him here, but he was glad all the same. Adam dropped his backpack and sat next to his father in the dirt. He hinged his arms out behind him and leaned back until he was comfortable.

"Hey, dad," Adam said.

"Hey, Adam," his father said.

The sun was going down in the distance. They watched the orange ball of fire descend, enjoying the serenity of the moment. In a few hours the stars would be out. If they made it that long. He hoped they did. He thought about the dinosaurs, and what their final moments were like, staring up at the sky as the Chicxulub asteroid approached. He found it funny, in a way, that if not for that asteroid, millions of years ago, he and the rest of humanity likely wouldn't exist. What smaller, more adaptable creatures would inhabit the Earth once humans were gone? Would cockroaches develop sentience and intelligence and take over the remaining buildings?

"How are your boys?" His father asked.

"They're good. They'll be with their families tonight."

"Good. Sad to not be with them?"

"Yes, but they will be okay."

"You raised them well."

Adam nodded, but said nothing.

"It's just you and me, then," his father said.

Adam's mother had died of breast cancer when he was only four, and Adam had only ever really known his father. Then, as if traumatic loss was genetic, Adam's own wife passed unexpectedly and far too early. He developed an understanding for what his father had gone through. It had been hard without his wife. So hard. Early on he'd felt abandoned and angry at her for leaving him and angry at the world for taking her away. Now, so many years later, he accepted it. He accepted that he was alone. It was his fate.

"Yup. Just you and me, dad. But I don't think I would have it any other way."

"Neither here."

Adam took out his phone. There were several more news alerts, but he didn't read them. Instead, he turned off the phone.

They sat in silence for the rest of the afternoon, staring off into the distance. Adam enjoyed the cool breeze against his skin and the brief moments of calm where the sun warmed him before disappearing behind clouds. Soon, the sky was a light purple, and the stars began blinking into existence. He'd always marveled at that. During the day, stars seemed to not exist at all, hidden behind the mirage that was the blinding sun. At night, when the sun went into hiding, reality was exposed, just in time for people to go to sleep and ignore it all.

"Dad, do you ever wonder if anyone else is out there?" Adam asked.

His father was silent for a while, thoughtful. "Not really," he finally said, "I guess it never really mattered to me. Everyone I need is here."

"I know, but you never just paused to think about it?"

"Hasn't everyone, at one time or another? I guess with the infinite size of space, I'm sure there are others out there."

"Actually, space being infinite is debated. It could actually have a finite size where it sort of... curves in on itself. But even so, if it is infinite, that's no guarantee for life."

"Oh really? Enlighten me." His father said.

"Okay, so I took a couple space courses in college, just for fun," Adam said. "In one of them, our professor explained that the there-has-to-be-life-because-space-is-infinite is an argument built on a common logical fallacy."

"It wasn't an argument," his father said, "Just a thought because you asked a question."

There was a hint of annoyance in his father's tone. His father was skeptical of "bookies" as he called them. People in colleges and universities, teachers, people that studied to learn instead of experienced. Adam didn't really understand why there had to be such resistance to professional learners. He figured it was an aspect of human nature, the gradual decay of trust. Once a person gets burned enough times, they learn to question everything unless they see it themselves with their own eyes. The unfortunate reality was that some things were impossible for someone to see on their own. And so society churned.

"Okay, I didn't mean you were, I'm just explaining. So this professor taught us that just because space is incredibly large, seemingly infinite, it doesn't mean that there has to be life beyond our planet. It's really the only thing I still remember from that class. It's funny how that works. I remember this and that the guy who sat next to me would start snoring halfway through class like clockwork. We'd sit in the far back, where the professor couldn't see us, because he was less likely to ask us questions.

"Anyway, the professor started by explaining that infinite space doesn't make the chance for life increase to infinity as well. The chance for life isn't accumulative as space expands. Chance for other life, whatever percentage it is, remains constant with scale. Just because one planet doesn't have life, it doesn't mean the next planet is more likely to have life, and the next, and the next, and so on. This means that there's still a chance for life outside of Earth to be zero, and it would always be zero for infinity, no matter how many planets are introduced."

He could see the disagreement in his father's face, those lines that formed along the eyes. His father had always been thoughtful and careful with his words. His father was a man that understood how easily meaning was lost when too much was said, and he would wait to speak, ensuring he had something valuable to say. He never forced words to fill the void of silence. Adam admired his father's ability for restraint.

"I guess I can see what your professor was thinking," his father finally said. "It makes sense. But I think there's another way to think about it, too."

"What's that?" Adam asked.

"Okay. It's just an idea, so I'm thinking out loud. Say we consider space to be infinitely large. Infinite space doesn't increase the chance for life, sure, but I think that's missing something."

"Like what?"

"So say something is infinite. In a way, that means that all possibilities must happen, or that anything that is not impossible has to happen, right? Because it's infinity. All things that are possible have to happen. It doesn't matter that there's not an accumulative chance for life on another planet, because it's not impossible for there to be more life out there. So if space is truly infinitely large, then there has to be more life out there somewhere. Right?"

"Well not really," Adam said, eager to prove his father wrong. It was like a game of chess. Against his father he usually lost, but he still found himself eager for the chance to win each time they played. "Just because you have infinite odd numbers, it doesn't mean you will ever come across an even number."

His father smiled, seeing the checkmate. "Yeah, but you declared a situation where it was impossible to have an even number, because all numbers were odd. In our world, it's not impossible for another planet to have life, however unlikely, because we have life here on our random planet in the middle of nowhere."

"Okay, my head is starting to hurt," Adam said, and his father laughed. Adam might have had more schooling under his belt, may have read more books than his father, but he'd never been able to outsmart him. It was another basic principle in the universe. All fathers knew more than their children, forever and always. Whether they were right or wrong, it was always true.

"I still don't know," Adam said, "Who knows, the universe probably isn't even infinitely large. I saw this documentary once that talked about how, due to the speed limit for light, we will only ever see a bubble of what's in the actual universe. This bubble is the size of how much time has passed in relation to the speed of light. It's a bubble defined by the inherent limitations of how light travels. Outside of this bubble, the rest of the universe could simply end. Or like I said earlier, it could curve in on itself like our planet does. Or it could truly go on for billions of light years in all directions. It is physically impossible for us to ever know, because we are limited to the laws of light and time."

"You sound frustrated by that."

"Yes, very. I want to know, and it means that I will never be able to know. We will never be able to know. There's a built in limitation to how much we are allowed to know. How bullshit is that?"

"Adam, I don't think it really matters. I think we learn to pass the time, not to truly know anything. The search, the journey, is what makes anything worth doing."

"I guess I don't agree. I want to know."

"I'm not sure that you do," his father said.

Adam didn't understand what his father meant, but didn't feel like asking, so silence fell over them. They watched the night sky, both admiring its beauty, taking in as much of it as they could in the time they had.

"Dad, do you know what the Drake Equation is?"

His father shook his head.

"It's an equation that can estimate the number of other planets in the universe that may have life, or can at least support life, based on I think seven or eight different parameters. I can't remember who came up with it, but I'd wager 'Drake' was probably somewhere in his name. The equation takes into account things like the number of stars, number of stars with planets, number of planets that can support life, and so on. I can't remember the exact different parts but that doesn't really matter. What I thought was cool was the concept, like we'd found a mathematical way to prove that there's other life out there.

"So here I research it further only to be frustrated to learn that it's basically a pointless equation. None of the data required to complete the equation can be determined with the technology we have today. Each part of it is unsolvable. Every single part. So to solve the equation, scientists have to put in best guesses based on what they do know, which isn't much. You should know Carl Sagan, right? Popular scientist when you were my age, back in the 80s or 90s."

"Yes, I know the name. He had a television show."

"He used the Drake equation to estimate roughly 1 million other highly intelligent civilizations out there in our Milky Way galaxy alone. Our cosmic backyard, so they say. In the scientific community, this is considered a pretty conservative estimate. More optimistic figures from other scientists have been as high as 150 million. Pessimistic figures have been as low as zero, no other civilizations out there, only us. How frustrating is that? We've invented the tools to know how to know, but not the tools to actually know. We're teased by potential."

"It does get us closer, though," his father said, "Each discovery leads to another, even if it doesn't feel that impactful today."

"I don't know, dad," Adam said, shaking his head, "To me, I read about it at first and felt hope. Then I felt like I was back at square one. We're either alone, or we're not. No new knowledge gained."

They were silent again, staring up at space, the impending doom forgotten as they wondered about what lay out there beyond what they could see. This had been common for both of them throughout life together, sitting silently in each other's presence. When Adam was a child, it bothered him because he wanted to talk to his father but didn't know what to say. When around his father, he would say a bunch of random things, saying really nothing at all, just filling in the silence in an attempt to connect. As Adam had grown, had gotten used to the silence, he found that being in his father's presence was enough, even if they didn't have much to talk about. Words weren't needed to relay the importance each had in the other's life.

The blinking stars above them were countless, some reddish in color, some light blue, most white. Some were large, blurred dots in the sky, and some were faint dots barely visible. It was impossible to consider each one in a single glance, and each one had planets possibly like Earth orbiting it. Dull rocks that neither of them could see, but still up there, far out of sight. Billions upon billions of objects far bigger in size than they could possibly comprehend. It was amazing. It was terrifying. It felt so out of reach.

"Dad, I got another one" Adam said, breaking the silence, "Have you heard of the Fermi Paradox?"

His father shook his head, then said, "I didn't know what we'd talk about as we waited, but I can honestly say that I didn't expect this."

Adam laughed. "You going to fall asleep on me?"

"Maybe," his father said with a smile.

"Anyway, the story that leads to this paradox starts all the way back in the 1800s. Nikola Tesla pointed a satellite at the sky and started listening for alien radio signals. From right here in Colorado Springs. At one point, he thought he caught a signal coming from Mars. He wrote a fun letter about it. 'Brethren!' he wrote 'We have a message from another world, unknown and remote. It reads: one... two... three....' was all the note said. Unfortunately, we know now that all he was hearing was cosmic background noise. Later in the 1900s, someone else, I can't remember his name, got excited because of a radio signal he caught that was much different than cosmic noise. He printed out the signal on a roll of paper, with a bunch of numbers that showed a kind of burst of noise. The scientist circled the burst on the printout and wrote 'Wow!', and it became known as the 'Wow! Signal'. Depressingly, it turned out to be nothing, though. At least as of what we know right now. Scientists have searched for the signal again in the same spot, but haven't found it. It could have been passing comets. It could have been a reflection of Earth's own signals off a piece of space debris. Still to this day we have satellites pointing up, trying to catch something, anything out there, but even with our technological advancements, it's still relative silence."

His father was nodding, catching on. "So, if there are millions of other intelligent life forms, as the Drake Equation might suggest, where are they?"

"Exactly. Fermi Paradox. Despite a seemingly infinite universe, where there should be life everywhere, we are living in a kind of great silence, a radio silence. We're not picking up anything else."

His father made a kind of groaning sound, then said, "I still don't think so. I bet we don't have the right technology yet, or other life forms communicate in different ways."

Adam said nothing, taking a page from his father's book, having nothing of value to say. He lost himself in the sky again, staring at a bright star above him, imagining what its orbiting planets might look like. He pictured artistic renditions he'd seen online, creations based on our collective knowledge of each planet's size and atmospheric composition. Scientists used light signatures each planet emitted to know fairly accurately the elemental makeup of newly discovered planets. Humans had advanced to the point that they could take accurate measurements from light years away, interpret those measurements, create a mock-up picture as if they were right up next to the planet, then send that off into the internet for someone like Adam to casually glance at without having to do any real work. It was incredible, and it humbled Adam, who hadn't contributed to society in any significant way. And yet, despite all humanity had learned, there were so many questions: How did it all begin? How would it end? Not just the Earth, but all of it, the whole universe. What was inside of a black hole? What was outside of the universe? Adam just wanted to know, and he was sad that he never would.

"You know, Adam," his father said, "There's something to be said about having a kind of faith. Not in any one person's version of God, but in there being some kind of higher purpose that will take care of us. Whether there are aliens out there, or whether we are one of a kind, it doesn't really matter."

"But there is no one taking care of us, dad. It's all chaos. All around us. On a macro level, as we wait for the world to end, and on the micro level, as each of us struggle to simply survive. I know what you're trying to say, but knowing should matter. More than it does. We should all want to know. But we don't. We don't value knowledge. Knowledge is a means to having more things, that's all."

Adam decided to change the subject before his father could challenge him, before he could try to blind him with optimism. "But let's back up a bit. You remember me saying that the Drake Equation convinced me that we're all alone? There's a part in the equation about knowing the number of civilizations like ours that send radio waves into space, and another about the length of time that civilizations are sending those messages into space. That final part always sends shivers down my spine."

"Why?" his father asked.

Adam looked over at his father, at the lines of age on his face. Adam, and his sons, would never know what it took to put that many lines on a man's face, that much history, that much experience. "Dad, have you ever thought about the insane age of the universe?" Adam asked, "About the absolutely bonkers time scale?"

"Haven't we all?" his father said.

"I mean really think about it. Deeply. I've struggled to fully picture it, to put things in a way that I can really comprehend. Not just 'really old' but how old. It's impossible. I've seen videos of people using string and football fields to measure it, and have seen the clock metaphors, but it still doesn't really help. I see the numbers, understand that they're massive, but I can't really get any closer than that to truly understanding the scale. For example, the universe is 13.8 billion years old, and the Earth is 4.5 billion years old, right? I see 13.8 and 4.5 and think, those are small numbers. But then you see the billions. It's like my brain doesn't really know what to do with that word. I can't compare it from one to the next.

"Think about people, about the human race. The United States is only about 250 years old. Your grandpa lived to be 94. He lived through over a third of US history, but to me he was just grandpa. On the other hand, US history seems ancient to me, as if it's always existed.

I know it didn't, that's it's a young country, but what I know and what I feel are such entirely different things." Adam paused, absorbing that thought before continuing. There was something there, two wires in his mind that wanted to connect, a realization of some sort, but the wires weren't long enough. He let it go. "Our ape-like ancestors walked Earth 2.4 million years ago, but they weren't what we'd consider intelligent. Their best tools were stones, fire, and crude hand axes. And I mean crude, like not even sharp. Chipped stone wedges. About 200 thousand years ago, those crude axes started becoming sharper tools, and 80 thousand years ago they had cutting blades made of stone. 50 thousand years ago the first languages began, and, because I was curious, 22 thousand years ago were the first fishing hooks."

"How do you remember all these numbers?" His father asked.

Adam continued, ignoring his father's attempt at derailing him with humor, "against all that, where would we consider the beginning of true human intelligence? Was it 2.4 million years ago, when we started making fire? 200 thousand years ago, when we started making better tools? 50 thousand years ago when we started communicating beyond grunts? Even that is still a really low level of intelligence, and it was just a fraction of the age of the Earth. Our higher level of intelligence has been around for even less time. Humans entered the bronze age around 5 thousand years ago. The digital age started only a 100 years ago. 100 years, dad. Technology has soared in those 100 years, and we're learning more about ourselves and where we live every day, but it was still less than an eye blink for the age of the planet, and barely visibly against the span of the universe.

"Anyway, I'm going somewhere with this. 200 thousand years ago, that's when the real breakthroughs started happening for us, I think. Crude tools started getting sharper, a little more advanced. That's the number I decided on when I was looking at this. Do you know how many times a span of 200 thousand years have happened during the 13.8 billion year old Universe? About 70 thousand times. The span of an intelligent race somewhere in the universe going from crude to advanced to eliminated has possibly happened 70 thousand times already. And they could have been wiped out long before they ever became intelligent enough to start sending out messages. And this is just looking at the time aspect, setting aside the immense size of space.

"How long, I wonder, for all traces of the human race to be completely wiped away once this is over? We act like we're here to stay, that the things we've built are eternal, but in the wide scale of time, it'll crumble and disappear before anything consequential in the Solar System ever happens. Stonehenge and the Pyramids are about 5 thousand years old, and consider their condition today. In 100 thousand years, much less a million, will anyone still evolving out there on another planet even know we were here?

"Consider Mars and Venus. They probably had life of some kind before us, or at least at the same time as ours first started. Maybe not intelligent, but still life. But the sun grew and super-heated Venus and now we can't see through the atmosphere to find evidence of life there. Mars lost its magnetic field and the atmosphere was blown away, meaning evidence of life there has been beaten, pulverized, and mixed into the red dust. Possibly, if we had landed on Mars, we could have dug into its layers and found something from millions of years passed. But for us to have to go to that extent, in our own backyard, what does it mean for the chances of life finding each other, while living?

"I think about that part of the Drake Equation a lot. Length of time between civilizations. It took us 100 years after moving into the digital age to reach our own destruction. 100 years. That's the window of time advanced civilizations have to speak to each other before they destroy themselves. In a universe nearly 14 billion years old, what is

100 years? How could we, or anyone that comes after us, ever hope to find anyone else? Maybe life is as common as our mathematics indicate, but common means nothing when life is fleeting against the expanse of time."

Adam stopped. He realized he was crying, his cheeks cold from the tears. His nose was dripping. He used the back of his hand to wipe the tears away. He felt so alone, more alone than he'd ever felt before, and deeply empty. After his wife had died, it had felt like nothing mattered. Nothing had value and everything was meaningless. Now, though, he realized even then there had been some hope, some hope for the human race, for his sons. Staring down a certain demise, the end of everything, it was now beyond meaningless. It all began, and it all would end. All without meaning.

He missed his sons, was sad that he'd not see them again, wished he'd done more to keep his family together. He had to remind himself that he was only human. He'd been struggling, had refused to talk to anyone, had even contemplated suicide a few times but couldn't commit to the act. He'd come to understand humanity's self-destructive nature at its most human level.

"I miss them so much, dad," Adam said, "I miss her, too, even now."

His father scooted closer to his son and wrapped him in an embrace. Adam dropped his head on his father's shoulders, feeling better under the pressure of his father's squeeze. When the weight of the world crushed him like an empty aluminum can, his father's presence built him back up and straightened out the dents. Adam wiped his eyes again and took a deep breath, feeling his heart rate slow. The wavering inside subsided.

He said, "I suppose we were lucky to have lived while we did."

"Yes, we were," his father said.

Adam closed his eyes and fell asleep.

2

When Adam awoke, it was later in the night. He knew this because the sky was a darker shade of purple, almost black, and because he was still alive. The air had gotten cooler, and he was shivering. He'd forgotten to bring blankets. The lights of Colorado Springs appeared to blink because of the miles between them, a sort of reflection of the stars in the sky above. Adam considered turning on his phone to check the time, but decided he didn't want to see updates in the news.

"Adam," his father said, "You're awake."

"Yes. I'm also cold," Adam said, involuntary shivers running down his back.

"What should we expect to happen, when it's time?" His father asked.

Adam spoke coolly, factually, having long ago accepted what was to happen. "We probably won't see anything when they do come. But depending on where they land, we'll see the bright light, and have a little time to talk before the impact waves reach us. This is based on what I've read, based on technology from a long time ago. Governments are more secretive about the power they have today."

"Is there anywhere to hide?" His father asked.

"Yes, there will be pockets of strategically unimportant places where some people could survive. But surviving the first few days of the onslaught is one thing. What comes next is something else."

"Why didn't you take cover somewhere, then, or try to leave?" Adam's father asked.

"I didn't see the point, really. I thought a lot about that. What I came to accept was that I don't want to live in the kind of world that will exist when this one ends. Survival brings out the worst in us." As he said this, he saw flashes of himself drunk and angry those first few years after she'd died. He'd been cruel and harsh, had isolated himself. To those around him, he'd probably been awful to be around. That's what survival looked like. He thought himself a decent man, and if trying to survive his wife's death had done that to him, what hope was there for a peaceful world once everyone was trying to survive a world in ruin?

"And you're certain that this is the end?" His father asked. "Are you sure we're not sitting here waiting for nothing?"

"I'm certain," Adam said. "You know, I've lived my entire life completely oblivious to this possibility. Did you know that that's a thing, though, for the younger generations? Baby boomers and older generations knew, they lived through the fear of the Cold War, but later generations didn't. Sure we had some wars in Iraq and Afghanistan, but it wasn't the same thing. There wasn't any real threat back home, safe in the states. We had no idea that this disaster had been bubbling under the surface for so long. We just assumed, took for granted, that we lived in a generally safe world, a world where everyone, all nations, all people, at least had the long term goal to enrich the human race. We figured we'd grown enough as a race to move on from war, assumed that everyone listened to history's lessons, assumed that everyone aspired for something more. But it was naive thinking, and we realized that as we grew up."

Adam felt a breeze ripple through his hair. He looked around, wondering if that slight uptick in wind meant anything, but didn't see anything.

"Here's the thing," he continued, "Surviving these initial blasts will only be temporary survival. No one will make it through the eventual end. It starts with a single nuclear weapon deployed. By any power, anywhere in the world, against another nation. Once that first nuke is used, it sets off a chain reaction. Retaliations begin, small ones of slightly greater force, so as to not appear weak. Attacks escalate, as countries can't back down else their governments face destruction from the offensive nation. Large scale responses begin, primarily targeting military bases. Hundreds or thousands of missiles begin fired, and these sort of attacks happen quickly, within minutes of each other in order for each country's military to gain a perceived upper hand.

"Do you know what military base is near Colorado Springs? I'm not talking about Fort Carson."

His father was nodding his head. The North American Aerospace Defense Command (or NORAD for short) was a publicly known nuclear command and control location roughly 10 miles south of Colorado Springs.

"Once we get to the point of launching full scale assaults on military targets, each side will try to strike down as many missiles out of the air as they can before they land. However, this is highly ineffective. The technology available to stop widespread missile attacks is still years out. Defensive technology always lags behind offensive technology. Think about that. Anyway, the next targets will be nuclear command and control bases and known weapons reserves. Further attacks from both sides will attack high population areas, cities that house the most population from both sides, military or not, the tactic being to slow the rebuilding phase following damage from the initial attacks.

"All of this initial phase of warfare could be over within a day, with millions of people killed. But this is based on research and simulations from another time, as I said earlier. Nuclear bombs today are far more advanced than what was used on Nagasaki and Hiroshima. Bombs today are like a thousand Hiroshima bombs packed into one missile. Colorado Springs, and us along with it, will be wiped out once those initial waves of attacks begin, certainly by the second waves if bases survive."

"Jesus," Adam's father said.

"Estimates indicate that in a single day, a nuclear war could kill more than 100 to 200 million people. And that's only the first day. The first day, dad. For comparison, over the six year span of World War 2, 50 million people died, and that's the largest death count of any war in human history.

"After that begins the truly horrific part. Within a month, Earth's natural weather systems begin carrying the nuclear fallout across the world, meaning eventually everywhere on Earth will become radioactive. After a year we're in what's called a Nuclear Winter. Debris in the air blocks out the sun. Crops die. Mass famine spreads. Below freezing temperatures become the new normal. It will take over a decade for the Earth to return to normal, but humans and most animals will already be long gone."

Far off in the distance Adam saw a bright light in the sky, a shooting star, dropping blindingly fast. He didn't see it make contact with the ground. A cloud of smoke rose up and took on the tell-tale mushroom shape as it grew. Adam admired that it looked almost exactly like a time lapse video of a growing mushroom. At the base of the upward-flowing cloud, Colorado Springs was reduced to dust and debris. 500 thousand people wiped out, Adam estimated. The blinking lights of the city and the sky were gone, replaced instead by the blinding light.

When sound finally accompanied the light, it was a bone crushing clap that rocked Adam's core, and the shock waves of the blast knocked him flat on his back. He'd expected an explosive sound, but it had been only one solid loud crack then soft rumbling like thunder.

He laid there for a while, listening to the passing echo of the explosion, waiting to smell his burning skin. It didn't happen. In fact, he felt little pain at all other than the concussive force of having been thrown onto his back and knocking his head on the hard rock of the mountain. The air felt uncomfortably warm, but he was not on fire.

He sat up and looked around. The sky, despite it being night, was unbelievably bright. His eyes burned, so he closed them and pinched them tight until the pain went away. He tried to peek through the slits of his eyes, looking for his father. In the flashes of his vision, he could see the mushroom cloud continue to climb upward in the distance. His heart raced. He checked his limbs, patted his arms and chest. Everything was there. He continued to look for his father, but couldn't find him. "Dad," he yelled, frantically looking around in snapshot glimpses. Everything was so bright. "Dad!"

"I'm here, Adam!" His father yelled back.

He followed the voice and found his father lying in the dirt some distance away. He ran to him, rocking from side to side as he did, his balance uneasy.

"Looks like we survived the first hit," his father said.

Adam knelt by his father, then calmed himself with deep breathing. His arms felt like rubber and he was trembling uncontrollably. It felt like his ears were bleeding. He rubbed the holes with a finger and pulled it away to confirm that he was. The red blood mixed with the dirt on his finger as it dripped.

The deep rumble of the explosion continued to carry in the distance. He felt an instinctual, momentary flight response. Run, now! His mind screamed at him. Before the next missile lands! He started to stand, but reality caught up. There was no escape now. Escape was a thing of the past. The new world had officially begun, and it wouldn't be a world for him.

"Dad, that's just the first strike," Adam said quietly, accepting again that his fate was sealed as he sat on the dirt. "There will be several strikes in this area to ensure total destruction of the location, if satellite imaging indicates that the target wasn't adequately destroyed. They can't take the risk for military survival in surrounding bunkers, which will need several strikes to penetrate."

"How much time do we have?"

"I really have no idea. Maybe minutes, maybe hours. Probably not days. If our military successfully destroys some of their missiles before they land, we might be safe for a little while longer."

"Okay," his dad said calmly, a beacon of stability against the backdrop of chaos.

"Okay," Adam said, and waited.

3

Some time passed as they sat among the rocks, breathing in the dust, letting their shock pass, and the cloud hanging over Colorado Springs continued to grow, ballooning outward into the surrounding area. Adam still struggled with the part of him that wanted to flee, felt that sense of impending dread. It was the same part of him that had kept him from committing suicide so many times before. He pushed against it, reminding himself that he knew what was coming, that this time he truly wanted it.

"You know, dad, I think this has been the inevitable conclusion for some time now. Not for me, I mean, but for the whole world. We've been lying to ourselves for a long time that we'd escaped this fate, but we only delayed the inevitable. We've always been eager to eliminate ourselves, have been waiting for the tools to do the job. We finally found them."

"It's easy to think that now," his father said, "but I don't think it's that simple, Adam. There are thousands of individual decisions that go into something like this. Hundreds of people are involved before the trigger is pulled. This wasn't inevitable. It could have been stopped."

"I'm not sure I agree."

"Why not?"

"Because this is all just a reflection of a micro-level condition at the macro scale. Every day, people we don't know make it through, but some people don't. People are consciously or subconsciously going nuclear on their lives for things they feel powerless to stop, feeling as though they have to just to survive. Each individual person is struggling with their inner demons, many making terrible decisions because of them, others making what seem like small choices that have big consequences because they're trapped in a never-ending self-induced cycle they're not aware of. Most of us aren't even thinking about the future, we're thinking about today, about how to survive today, thinking about how to just make it through just one more goddamn day. Forget how our brains can't comprehend the massive time scale of the universe. It's barely equipped to fully understand and plan for tomorrow. Each of us is built to self-destruct.

"I have this news app on my phone. It has this feature where you can set your location and it'll compile local news. So to pass the time sometimes, I'd set my location to small towns all over the states. You see, we're numb to violence at a national or global level, almost accept it, but when things happen in our own backyard it's cause for major concern. So I like to follow and see what gets posted, what's happening in that small community I'm out of reach with, and see how they're coping. I enjoy them because of just how human the stories are, these tiny little reflections of minuscule events.

"I saw this news story from a town in Minnesota. A young boy watched his older brother drown in the lake just outside of town. Could you imagine? I thought about watching one of my own sons drown, and it made me feel sick to my stomach. What if it was a sibling? But this story wasn't about the first brother, but the second. The younger brother ended up drowning the next year on the same lake. He'd become obsessed with the idea that a lake monster, a lake monster, had killed his brother, and was desperate to find it."

"Do you think the monster was real?" Adam's father asked.

"I don't know, but I don't really think the monster matters, you know? That boy didn't need to die. That's what I'm trying to explain. The boy killed himself by going back out on that lake because he couldn't move on.

"In another, a particularly brutal story, a man tried to kill his ex wife in their child's bedroom. She ended up getting away from him, apparently by stabbing him with her keys a few times. Police entered the home to arrest him for the assault and found him lying on a pile of his ex wife's clothing in that very bedroom, dead. Apparently he bled out from the stab wounds. That was an interesting story, because he shouldn't have been able to bleed out from the superficial cuts the keys left. But that's beside the point. He tried to kill his wife, ended up dying, simply because he couldn't move on from their past.

"One of the worst ones I found was of a young man who killed his pregnant girlfriend. He apparently wasn't ready to be a parent. He beat the girl to death with his fists, pounded her head into the ground. And he wasn't finished there. He ripped the baby from her belly, presumably just to ensure the child was dead. Neither the young man nor the dead baby has been found yet. His mother was quoted in the article saying she didn't believe her son capable of murder, but that he had been a troubled child ever since his father had died in a car accident."

Adam started to laugh. "That child's name, the boy that grew up and murdered that girl? William. Fun tidbit, did you know that the name William means 'strong-willed warrior'? Seems fitting for a boy that survives a car accident, but for a man that murders someone innocent? Brutal."

"Adam, enough." His father said, "Sometimes I think your pessimism makes you cold."

Adam nodded his head, said, "I'm sorry, you're right."

His father didn't reply.

Adam continued, "All I'm saying is that these people destroyed their lives because they couldn't escape their own minds, their own humanity. We struggle to ask for help because we'd rather destroy ourselves with pride rather than admit defeat. That's why I think we've always been doomed. Even at that individual level, survival brings out the worst in us. Ending the world through nuclear warfare isn't much different than what we're already doing to ourselves every day anyway. As the saying goes, our greatest enemy is ourselves."

4

Adam was lying down, staring at the sky. The blinding light had finally cleared, but he couldn't see the stars anymore, as if the bombs had eliminated them from existence, too. In reality, the dust from the onslaught had created a blinding layer in the atmosphere, separating people on Earth from the rest of space indefinitely. The night sky looked wrong without the stars, and it made Adam feel uneasy. Yet, if he were being honest with himself, it wasn't only the weirdness of the sky making him feel this way. It was the uncomfortable truth that had been bubbling up to the surface ever since the bombs first hit. He was tired of hiding from it, and this close to death, didn't feel it was worth it anymore.

"Dad, I lied to you earlier," Adam said. "I never called the boys."

"I know," his father said.

Of course his father already knew. His father, this version of him at least, knew everything. This father was a re-creation, an optic and synaptic model of what his father used to look like, but real enough for Adam to talk to. A defense mechanism. His father had passed away several years ago from colon cancer.

"The first few days after she died are a complete blur," Adam said. "I didn't know who I was anymore, what my purpose was, what I wanted to do. In a blink of an eye a year had slipped by, and the boys along with it. They didn't call anymore, didn't come and see me. I'm not sure if I scared them away, or if everything was too hard for them to deal with. Maybe a bit of both. Every once in a while, I've thought about calling them, but I kept stopping myself. At first I didn't call them because I was nervous and didn't know what to say. Then, after a while, I didn't call because it felt like too much time had passed. I was perpetually searching for both a reason to call and a reason not to call. Now I'm stuck. Stuck because I could never figure out how to get today to the point I want for the future. Now that'll be our permanent state. Me here, forever alone, dying with my boys in thoughts only, them never knowing what happened to their father."

"You're not alone," his father said. "You need to know that."

Another missile hit the earth in the far distance, too far for Adam to feel its impact, but close enough to hear the rumbling. Adam glanced at his father. He could see him, lying there against the red dirt of the mountain, but the apparition was fading, his mind accepting reality.

"There's another hypothesis about intelligent life," Adam said, changing the subject, "It's called the Rare Earth Hypothesis. It hypothesizes that the conditions to support life are incredibly rare. The planet has to be just right, not too hot and not too cold. It has to be in just the right location within a galaxy, in an area of low energy. It has to be the right distance from the right cool and low-energy, long-living star. It has to have the right arrangement of rocky planets and gas giants to deflect comets. It has to have a stable orbit, and be the right size to maintain a magnetic field. It has to have a large moon to provide a stable climate and the right atmosphere for breathable air. It has to be old enough to support the level of evolution needed for intelligent life."

There was a larger explosion hit in the distance, but closer. The sky was bright with light again. The missiles hitting now were smaller, but there were more of them, the sky alight with hell fire. Adam thought again about the paintings of the dinosaurs staring up into the sky as the Chicxulub meteor had fallen. In each painting was a Tyrannosaurus Rex looking up at the sky, staring at what would inevitably be the end of life as it knew it. Look at me, Adam thought, empathizing with a dinosaur.

"I think about that theory, too," Adam continued, "And I know for certain that humans, here on Earth, are all there is out there. Forget the Drake Equation, the Fermi Paradox, the great expanse of time and space. There were too many incredibly unlikely things that needed to happen in order for us to exist. Too many incredibly unlikely things for us to live with our immense technological advancements for only 100 years. We were the one anomaly, the one chance occurrence for intelligent life, the one opportunity to know and to understand. We were the universe's mind as it tried to understand itself, and it took 13.8 billion years of chaos to create us. Here we are, the universe's ungrateful children, soon to be no more. Given a gift we don't know how to properly use."

"Adam," his father said. It was a voice in his mind now, no object available for ventriloquism, "Everything is a choice. Humanity finding life on another planet won't make you feel any less alone."

"What do I do, dad?" He was crying now, alone on the mountain, waiting for the end. "What do I do?"

Adam's father flooded his son's mind with images, memories he'd long forgotten. The first of his father waking him up in the morning, shaking him from his bed, telling him it was time to get ready for school. The second of the way his father stood in the low-lighting of the kitchen as he drank his coffee and listened to the news. He remembered the taste of the cigarette smoke in the truck as his father drove him to school. He remembered the rough etching of his father's cheek as he hugged him and told him, "Have a good day, buddy," before driving away from the front entrance of that very school. He remembered the creak of the truck door as he was picked up from school, his father smiling, saying "Hey, buddy, how was your day?" He remembered his father's laugh as they watched television together, could hear his father's voice as he explained to Adam what was happening in the movie. Adam knew the movie well, because his dad watched it over and over, an action flick with absolutely no meaning at all, yet Adam would watch the movie years later and would remember his father because it brought him back to a certain feeling. He remembered his father teaching him skills that he'd undervalued at the time. He remembered to hold the drill up high, level with the angle of the screw so as to not strip it, and to apply even pressure. He remembered how to lay shingles, lining them up just below the tar line, with five nails across to hold them down and no more. He remembered lessons that made no sense at the time, but did now, about load bearing beams and about how to frame walls. He remembered his father telling him to take a breath when he was angry, that good things never came from anger, and not to lash out at those around him, a lesson he was told when he'd broken his knuckles after a fight. He remembered his father telling him he loved him, and that he was proud of him, after he graduated from high school and moved away from home in search of his first real job. He remembered that great big smile on his father's large, balding head each time he would come home to visit, as Adam brought his future wife home to meet the family. He remembered his father's tears of joy when he met his first baby grandson, then again when he met the second.

In those memories, Adam thought that maybe his dad was right, that the importance of life had nothing to do with the whole, and everything to do with the individual. Life in the universe may be fleeting and Earth itself forever alone, but Adam's life held infinite importance to his sons, just as his father had been infinitely important to him. For the first time in many years, not knowing the truth felt okay.

Adam fell to his knees as he looked up into the sky, feeling over-whelmed with joy, guilt, purpose, and more. He stared into the burning sky as he was flooded with a sense of emotion that he hadn't allowed himself to feel for years. The bright light of death sketched lines across his face as missiles flew across the sky, and he breathed in deeply, pulling in the corrupt air around him until his lungs burned with the fury he felt. He screamed. He screamed until his lungs ached and his throat was torn with microscopic tears in the tissue.

When the emotion was finally spent, he wiped his eyes. He'd start with California, which was a little bit closer, then he'd go to Florida. He didn't know where he'd physically find them in the new world that awaited them, but he would, because that's what life was. Survival wasn't the new world, it was the only world that had ever been, and people made it a bearable experience.

"I miss you so much, dad," Adam said to his father, who was gone but never far, as fathers tend to be.

Holding dearly onto his new optimism for life, Adam ran to his car, desperate to leave the rock before more missiles struck. When the missiles did strike, Adam felt nothing. He didn't feel his skin catch fire as it sizzled, bubbled, boiled, and dripped from his body. He didn't feel his organs burst, one by one like popcorn, blood cooking and turning to carbon, ash, and dust. He didn't feel his bones disintegrate into a powder with the impact of the passing shock wave. Instead, in his mind, the final thought locked in permanence with his body's final resting spot, was a singular, eternally repeating mission:

Boys, I'm coming home.

"When my son looks up at me and breaks into his wonderful toothless smile, my eyes fill up and I know that having him is the best thing I will ever do." –Dan Greenberg

"A father doesn't tell you that he loves you. He shows you."

–Dimitri the Stoneheart

PREVIEW: FLESH PARTY

The following is a preview of the title short story in Jordan Thiery's next collection, *Flesh Party: Five Monstrous Horror Stories*.

The woman was lying in the tub, her long hair floating around her body as blood flowed from her arms. The once hot water had quickly begun to feel cold.

Earlier that night had started the same as any other. She'd been feeling down, an "intense low", as the therapist would describe it. She hadn't been taking her mood stabilizers. She'd felt tired, bored, and disappointed with how her life had turned out. She'd tried distracting herself from negative thoughts, but failed. Her apartment was dark, quiet, and insistent, and it worked in collusion with thoughts fueled by loneliness.

As the onslaught of her thoughts ran rampant, she'd done as her therapist had recommended. She'd tried to find something to do, something to keep herself busy, something that gave her a sense of joy. But this task felt impossible when every action felt like work. She'd tried reading, but the swirling void in her gut distracted her. The words on the page blended together into a blurry smudge, and behind glazed eyes, hateful thoughts returned. She was worthless. She was nothing. She was waste and failure. No one wanted her. No one valued her.

The door of her apartment was closed to the world. Only a twist of a wrist, fingers gripping the door knob, separated her from the people outside. But once outside where would she go? She'd had no one to see, no one that wanted to see her. Would she shop, wandering stores aimlessly, looking at objects she didn't have the energy to use, with barely enough money to purchase?

She wondered why she didn't deserve happiness. People around her were finding the things she desired (a spouse, a home, a career, marriage, children, a family pet). Yet here she was in her studio apartment, a waitress without any career trajectory, unable to find a long term partner that cared even marginally about her well-being. What was so wrong with her that she didn't get to have what everyone else stumbled effortlessly into? It hurt, those feelings growing like a void in her gut. Worst still, despite their increasing frequency, it seemed she couldn't become calloused to them. She didn't want to live anymore if this was what life was destined to be.

She'd taken out her phone and texted an older man. It was someone she'd been seeing. She texted him often, but he usually didn't text back unless he was in the mood for *things*. She knew she shouldn't talk to him, knew he'd never see her as a person of value. It didn't matter. Spending nights alone in her apartment was worse, with that hateful void spinning, swirling, growing inside her. She'd decided she would offer her body for a few hours of companionship. It would give her a break from the black hole consuming her.

When the man had arrived, she'd held him back for as long as she'd dared, pretending she wanted to watch a movie and talk. He'd been eager for *things*, but was willing to play the game for a little while. For a time, she'd had companionship. They'd been nearly friends, it seemed, as he'd smiled and made jokes.

Eventually his desire had become unbearable and he was in her ear, kissing her cheek, hand down her sweatpants. She hadn't wanted to do it, not so soon, knowing he'd leave once the deed was done, but he'd been so insistent. She'd tried getting up, tried offering food or beverage, but he'd grown agitated, would leave if she didn't complete the transaction. So she'd taken off her shirt, raising her hands up high and lifting slowly, teasing him until her breasts were exposed.

He'd been drooling for her. He'd taken her, and then they were on her bed. He'd played with her sloppily, just enough to get her wet and no more. He'd finished on her belly, and she'd smiled at him. She'd asked if he'd like to watch a movie, but the man was cold now, had to go home and get to bed because he worked in the morning. She'd begged him, but he'd told her to stop being clingy or "this thing" wouldn't work out. He'd left, the apartment again quiet.

She'd laid on the couch, still naked after wiping away his mess. The smell had hung in the air as she watched the flickering images on the television, the smell making her long for someone to lie with after sex, to talk to, to cuddle with, to fall asleep with. She'd texted the man again, telling him she hoped he'd have a good day at work tomorrow. He didn't text back. It would be a few more days before he wrote back, before he became desperate enough to settle for her again.

Was any of this worth it? She'd thought, as the void, that swirling emptiness, returned. No, she didn't think it was.

She'd gone to the bathroom and started a bath of hot water. She'd stared at herself in the mirror as the steam creeped up around the edges of the glass. She'd tried to admire her body but couldn't. She was too frail, too bony. Her tits were too small. She was short and her face lacked features. She had fat hands and feet. Her hair was thin, straight, and greasy looking. It was the color of watered down period blood.

From atop the mirror she'd grabbed one of the razor blades from a pile, hidden underneath the vanity lights. There was no reason to hide them, no one else in the apartment to hide them from, but still she did. She hid them from herself, in a way, hidden from a reality she didn't want to acknowledge. She'd looked at the lines covering the insides of her thighs, and considered for a moment. Then she'd looked at her arms, her clean arms, open slates. She'd taken the blade with her and stepped into the tub.

The heat had been scorching, had hurt her skin for a moment, as if she were cooking, but her body adjusted. She'd looked at the blade, examining it as it shone in the light, still thinking. Before she could change her mind, she'd placed the blade against her wrist and pushed, pushed until the blade broke flesh. The blood started to pour. She'd pulled the blade down once more, vertically along her wrist, and more blood escaped. She'd felt nauseated at the sight of it, felt a rush of vertigo. It was more blood than she'd ever seen in her life. She'd switched hands and done the same to the other wrist, this time with some difficulty as her grip weakened. She'd dropped her hands into the water, and the blood and the bath water mixed. The blood had started as a stream of red floating to the surface, then became a pinkish color as the blood thinned in the water. Soon the bath water had become a deep red as her vision began to fail her.

Now she closed her eyes, letting that old life go, waiting for the moment to come. She was fading out, fading into whatever came next. Her nerves were ocean waves of sensation, in and out, in and out, thoughts flowing from her as the silence swirled around her. She felt peace. It was ending. She'd felt pain for the last time, and it was pain under her own control. Behind her closed eyes she could feel the world leaving her. No, she corrected the thought, she was leaving the world.

In the silence she unexpectedly heard sounds and wondered if they were the sounds of what came next. She'd expected permanent silence, but instead heard movement. She opened her eyes. She was still in her bathroom, the lines of existence wavy, vision unsteady.

Then she saw them, tall and elegant. The first bent down to pick her up and out of the water while a second watched. She decided they were angels, here to take her away. Her blood continued to flow from her body, pooling on the ceramic tiling below her as the first angel held her for the second to examine.

The second angel seemed to be judging her, eyes boring into hers. Was she worthy of a gift, at least the gift of death? Of peace? Of an existence vacant of pain? The second angel placed a hand on the young woman's face, closing her eyelids and covering her nose and mouth. She was in darkness again, listening, her sensations continuing to fade.

Then she felt the cutting begin. Not the cutting she'd done to herself. No, this was a flaying of her skin. She tried to move, but was too weak. The angel, the devil, continued to hold her eyes closed as the other sliced at her body. She felt deep cuts across her chest, into her arms, into her legs, seemingly all at once. She wanted to scream out but was too weak to do so.

Finally the pain met its peak and everything faded out. It had happened. She was finally calloused.

She would die this way, she realized. Not in peace and silence, but in the hands of devils tearing her flesh from her bones, listening to the sounds of leather ripping from inside the blackness. But what was the difference from this death to life, really?

The young woman felt what must have been true death, as all grew silent and still around her, the blackness reaching a level of completeness.

Then the devils rebuilt her.

ABOUT THE AUTHOR

Jordan Thiery lives in North Dakota with his wife and four children. Despite what the stories in this book might suggest, he loves being a father. He is a new part-time author and happily works full-time with Amazon.com. *Our Greatest Enemy* is his first published work. His next publication will be a second collection of short stories: *Flesh Party: Five Monstrous Horror Stories*. To stay up-to-date on current projects and future publications, visit http://jordanthiery.com. Social media accounts are listed on the website.

9 798330 242306